The House In

by Helen Cardwell

Copyright @ Helen Cardwell

Helen Cardwell has asserted her right under the Copywright, Designs and Patents Act 1988 to be identified as the author of this work.

The characters featured in this book are fictional. Any resemblance to persons living is purely coincidental.

ISBN 978-1-4717-3069-6

This book is sold subject to the condition that it shall not, by way of trade or otherwise, be lent, resold, hired out, or otherwise circulated without the publisher's prior consent in any form of binding or cover other than that in which it is published and without a similar condition including this condition being imposed on the subsequent publisher.

First published in Great Britain in 2012 by the author.

www.publishnation.co.uk

The Mournsby Prophesy.

A Grey shroud of sorrow, of loss and of pain,
Shall cover the village bearing grief's name.
Undending,
Unbroken,
The innocent cries shall silent remain,
Until deaths grace returns there again.
With a touch of a hand,
The gates they will part,
A beginning to the end of shadow and dark.
Then journey on through,
The Keeper of Bones own domain,
And onto the passage,
Where those who are lost have been lain.
Beyond lies a danger,
And many souls it has claimed,
Who can only be saved,
When what was taken,
Is theirs once again.
But do not rush to this task my friend,
For only the one,
Who is born of the dead,
Can break the curse of the House at Larchend.

Contents

Chapter One; No Escape
Chapter Two; New Arrivals
Chapter Three; Unsettling In
Chapter Four; A New Mystery
Chapter Five; New Discoveries, New Friends
Chapter Six; Welcome Home
Chapter Seven; Mrs Barrowhyde
Chapter Eight; Shadows and Lights
Chapter Nine; A Story Shared
Chapter Ten; Looking To The Past
Chapter Eleven; The Full Story
Chapter Twelve; The One Born Of The Dead
Chapter Thirteen; Death Returns
Chapter Fourteen; Consequences

Chapter One
No Escape

"One, two, three, four, five…" The door slammed violently against the bedroom wall as the girl tore through it onto the landing, her lungs heaving as they tried to draw in sufficient air. The shadow that flittered across the window of the room she had broken out of told her it was time to move. She ran for the staircase, her footsteps thundering loudly on the thin red carpet that had, not so long ago, seemed so warm and welcoming. Too late she found out what it really was; a scarlet pathway to doom.

Stumbling down the last few steps as her feet tangled themselves together in haste, she tumbled onto the hall floor. She did not have time for the pain to register. IT was there. A cold, cruel laughter mocked her, revealing how much its owner enjoyed the distress being caused.

The child, who could have been no more than 7 years old, crawled hurriedly towards the small table on the other side of the hallway as fast as her shaking limbs could drag her, and she scurried under it.

From her hiding place she could see the doorways to every room on that level of the building, yet the table meant she was not able to be observed by anyone outside the house. Despite how terrified she felt, the girl could not shed a single tear as the seriousness of her situation set in. How could a simple game end like this?

Her heart missed several beats as the noise of claw like fingers scraped along the outer walls. She held her breath as the voice that had lured her to this place with words of happiness and joy neared.

"Ninety eight, ninety nine, one hundred. Coming, ready or not!"

All was silent. The only sound to reach her was that of her own heart as it thumped against her ribs. She had to find a way out.

From her place of sanctuary, she noticed the stalking shadow moving about at the rear of the premises. This was it; her one chance. It was now or never.

With every cell in her body quivering, the girl made for the front door. It wasn't until then, as she reached for the handle, the truth about how dire her situation was became known. Stunned by what she saw from the hall window, she could not help but become frozen to the spot.

She had entered the house earlier that evening as dusk was setting in. The sun had transformed the evening sky into a vibrant sea of orange making the trees that lined the avenue appear black against it. The lights had started to come on in the houses as if summoned to work by the birds with their evening serenades. These things, and everything else familiar to her, had gone. A void of emptiness had swallowed them all up.

Desperately, the girl strained her eyes, hoping to pick out a house or car that was recognizable, but there was nothing to be seen. As she stood looking, in a dazed state of confusion, another shock was delivered when the window she was gazing out of was filled by a huge pair of eyes that peered in, locking onto their prize immediately.

So sudden and terrifying was the sight that the poor child could not help but jump back. Her shoes caught the rug which lay behind her, and once more she found herself crashing to the floor. The face at the window grinned triumphantly.

"You said you wanted a new home, one where you were wanted." A low creak echoed out from behind the girl, who could not decide where to look. She did not want to take her eyes off the fiend at the window but she feared what new monster was approaching from behind. She scrambled over to the wall, pressing her back flat against it, her eyes moving swiftly between the window and the area where the noise had come from, determined not to be caught off guard.

In the centre of the hall a door swung open of its own accord, revealing a vast gaping hole leading underneath the house, and from within it the sounds of dozens of dragging footsteps headed towards her.

"You wished for a family who wanted you, well here it is."

Marching up from the unseen stairs appeared line after line of children. Boys and girls of all ages from five to ten years of age, dressed in a variety of styles dating back more than a hundred years. The only thing they had in common was the vacant expression which was fixed to each of the gaunt faces that edged nearer, arms outstretched, ready to greet their new sister.

"Welcome to your new home," the voice outside cackled as it started to move away.

"No, don't. Don't leave me!" the girl begged as she tried to escape the lost children who were almost upon her. She banged desperately on the window, only stopping when the light from the door of the room outside her prison opened, flooding the area in its harsh, yellow glow, revealing the truth about where she was.

Out of the window, where houses and trees had been lined up neatly beside their lawns, there stood instead a dingy bookcase, covered in cobwebs. The grass had been replaced by a dusty table on which the doll's house she was a captive in had been stood on since the first day she laid eyes on it. The hairs on her neck stood up as the cold embrace of her fellow residents grew closer.

"Don't leave me here," she pleaded with her deceiver, who appeared silhouetted against the doorway of the attic, with the girl's own motionless form at their side.

"Leave you? I'll never leave you. You belong to me now, and will be mine for eternity."

The figure left, closing the door behind it, shutting out the last radiant beams of mortality, leaving the girl to her fate. The lights of the doll house flickered as the first of the cold fingers reached out and touched the girl's shoulder.

"Welcome sister," the voices whispered together. The lights of the doll's house went out, another groan was heard as the door closed and the attic was still again.

Chapter Two

New Arrivals

The car radio gave a final spurt of static and fell silent. No amount of twiddling the dials could stir the slightest sign of life from it. Rather like the miles of emptiness around them Elinor thought. Just as the control panel of the stereo could not find any trace of civilisation, the scenery they made their way through could not raise any joy in the girl's heart. She pulled her mobile phone out of her pocket, wondering if it might have a signal; she was disappointed again.

"There's no point in trying any of your gadgets around here. It's a dead zone." Elinor gave a sarcastic huff.

"You took the words right out of my mouth."

"Oh, Elinor, Please don't," Aunt Sarah sighed. "We had no choice but to move. There was nothing left after the divorce and this was the only job I was certain to get, not to mention that paid enough to support the three of us."

Elinor resumed the sulk she had been tending with great dedication during the five hour drive that took her further away from her old life and closer to the new one awaiting her. Actually, she had been brooding over the move for a good deal longer than that. Six weeks, three days, eighteen hours and twenty four minutes to be accurate, ever since her aunt broke the news they had to move so she could take up the position of secretary which her brother had offered her at his law firm in the city.

Annoying as it was to leave the town she had grown up in, as well as her friends, Elinor was quite excited at the thought of living in a big city. However, this hope was quickly dashed by the announcement that, even with the generous wage her brother was paying, there was no way the three of them, Elinor, Aunt Sarah and her daughter, Sophie, could afford a property in the city. Instead, she had found a cheaper house in a small village about fifteen miles outside of the city.

Any remaining hopes about her having some sort of social life had also been swiftly squashed as they drove through miles of fields, hedgerows and tree lined lanes. There was absolutely nothing to be seen, The most exciting moment in the whole journey was when a rabbit scampered out in front of the car, and everyone quickly placed bets on whether Sarah would hit it or not. Luckily for the rabbit, Aunt Sarah was a cautious driver, which allowed the poor creature to escape in one piece, though its heartbeat must have increased dramatically at the close call.

After what seemed like forever, the wild hedges gave way to their well-maintained cousins that ran along recently cut grass verges. The road widened slightly too, and even had markings now it was large enough to be split into two distinctive halves. There was also a noticeable drop in the number of potholes for the car to plunge into. Civilisation was nearby.

The car rounded a long, sweeping curve in the lane, which required ever more turns of the steering wheel to manoeuver the car around it, when there it was; the sign post announcing to the tired passengers they had almost arrived at their destination.

'Welcome to the village of Mournsby,' the sign declared in its old fashioned script. Elinor thought never in the history of the entire world had a place been more suitably named, nor so accurately summed up how she felt about the situation she had been dropped in. Aware of her aunt watching her, as if reading her mind, Elinor gave an indignant stare in return.

"I never said a word," she pleaded in her own defence, though it must have been obvious how she felt.

Aunt Sarah turned off the main street and onto a narrow road overhung by ancient Oak trees. So far, there had not been a single building of any description to be seen, but finally, through a gap in the branches, a dark slate roof flashed into view briefly, and as the tunnel of trees was exited, a cluster of houses burst into view.

They were old buildings, most of which still had many of their original features. Lead lined windows winked in the sunlight at the new arrivals passing by the front doors with their stained glass panels and brass door knockers. It was like something out of a story book. Ahead they saw a house with a middle aged woman stood on its lawn, who was unmistakably on the look-out for someone.

"This one is ours," Sarah said, unable to hide the mix of relief and exhaustion that could be heard in her voice as she pulled the car to a halt. Sarah left Elinor and Sophie to force their journey bound limbs out of the vehicle, which they did with several groans of pain being released as kinks were worked out of legs and spines. Sarah headed towards the waiting woman, who was making her way down the path to greet the new tenants.

"Mrs Braxton," Sarah said with forced cheerfulness, for she was especially tired from the drive. "I do hope you've not been waiting long."

The woman, who was quite plump with light brown hair that was flecked with grey, smiled warmly at her.

"Mrs Cutter. How nice to meet you in person at last. It is nice after all those phone calls to be able to put a face to the name. Well, here it is, End Cottage. I hope it lives up to your expectations. Though, why you need such a large place is beyond me. Are you sure you won't rattle around in there on your own?" Sarah looked puzzled at the remark, which in turn confused Mrs Braxton. "Is something wrong, Mrs Cutter?" Sarah laughed softly.

"Oh, no. It's just that, well I'm not on my own." Sarah had barely finished explaining herself when a look of shock crossed the face of the other woman.

It was as if she had seen a ghost materialize before her. Sarah turned to see what had caused this reaction, and found Elinor and Sophie behind her. They had finally struggled free from the car, and assuming the handing over of the house keys was about done, had joined Sarah on the path leading up to the house.

"Is something wrong?" Sarah enquired, concerned by how pale her landlady had become.

"You didn't say you had children," Mrs Braxton answered, in a voice that was full of dread.

"Yes, I did. I told you their names too. This is Elinor, and hiding behind her legs is Sophie." There was no denying the girls had taken the woman by surprise. The colour had all but vanished from her cheeks, her voice was strained and she seemed to be suffering from some inner torment.

"Oh, well. It must have slipped my mind. They are easy to forget after all."

"What? Peoples names?"

"No," Mrs Braxton said, "children."

The words hung heavily in the air, but whatever haunted the woman left as quickly as it had come, and Mrs Braxton became her former happy self.

"Well, I don't want to take up anymore of your time. You've had a long trip and will want to get settled in for the night. Do call in at the shop soon. And if there is anything special you want ordering in, just ask. Mr Braxton always goes out of his way to help the locals." She handed over the keys to Sarah, then, with one final look of puzzlement at Elinor and Sophie, she bid the family farewell.

They stood together on the edge of the lawn in front of the grey stoned house. To Elinor, it looked less welcoming than the properties they had driven past, even though it was pretty much identical in every way.

Through the thick mass of Ivy that climbed across most of the stonework, it's huge, old windows stared down at them almost accusingly. The garden path ran from the street, up the side of the grass and to the front door which was painted in the deepest shade of blood red paint imaginable. The house itself was made up of three floors; the ground floor, a first floor and one where the attic must have been originally.

As it was summer, the garden was alive with flowers and plants of every colour. They only had one neighbour, for their house was the last on the street, but down its spare side ran a wide track-way, though it was apparently rarely used as it was barely visible amid the overgrown weeds that grew around it. Also, largely hidden from view thanks to the out of control foliage, was an old stone wall that followed the route of the track, at least so far as the eye could see, which was overhung by the branches of the trees that grew on its far side. The wall and trees combined made it impossible to see what lay beyond.

The house that was to be their new home was very ordinary. An ordinary house in an ordinary village, yet there was something about the place that set Elinor's nerves on edge. It was stupid she knew, but to her it felt like the place was waiting, waiting for something to happen. She shivered despite the warm sun shining down on her.

"Well, here we are kids," Sarah sighed. "Welcome to your new home."

Chapter Three

Unsettling In

Everyone was relieved Sarah had taken a house that came fully furnished as they lugged the last of the boxes into the hall. Not that she had had much choice in the matter. Almost everything from the house she owned with her husband, Max, had been sold in order to cover the huge debts he had run up, unbeknown to his wife. It wasn't until he took off with his secretary that Sarah discovered he had neglected to pay the bills on their home in order to fund his secret life. Sarah's brother, who always thought it best to look on the bright side of things, told her she was, in truth, quite fortunate to have got off so lightly. Had Max not lost his job when he did, it had to be wondered what he would have done next behind his wife's back.

Though people would not have believed it, Elinor did feel sorry for Sarah and Sophie. The divorce might have cost the three of them their home but that was all Elinor had lost. The others fared worse. Sarah had lost her husband, even though he was a lying, cheating, good-for-nothing loser, and Sophie had seen her father for what he was. Elinor was the one person who had been more than a little overjoyed the day Max packed his bags and left. She had hated him for as long as she could remember, and it was entirely mutual.

Max never attempted to conceal the fact he despised having to keep the 16 year old Elinor fed, clothed and housed. To him she was a brat, a burden, and had been since the day she came to live with them.

"You should have put it in an orphanage," Elinor heard him say to Sarah one time. "She wasn't our responsibility, but no! You had to bring her here, like some stray puppy you found dumped by the roadside."

"Did you really expect me to abandon her, give her over to strangers? Elinor is the last connection I have to Eve, and I would not break that for anyone or anything."

In fact, Sarah was not being entirely accurate, for neither her mother nor father were her natural parents. They adopted Elinor as a baby. She knew the circumstances around her birth parent's death's and her subsequent adoption, for Max enjoyed pointing out how she had no connection to any living being in the world. Both had been killed in a terrible car crash, and Elinor was adopted by Eve and Ben, who was her uncle on her mother's side. Sadly, they too were snatched away from the girl in tragic circumstances.

Sarah was Eve's step-sister and following the untimely deaths of Elinor's adoptive family, took in the child and tried to raise her as her own, a task made virtually impossible by Max. He insisted Elinor call them Aunt Sarah and Uncle Max, rather than by their first names alone. If anyone made the mistake of thinking her to be the couple's daughter, Max would instantly correct them, a habit Elinor picked up, and did automatically herself whenever the error occurred. As for money, well! He never stopped whining about how much it cost to 'keep' her. Elinor frequently thought she sounded more like an unwanted pet than a human being. She regularly received lectures on how much his family had to go without in order to put clothes on her back and food on her plate. Sophie, despite being just seven years old, was told on several occasions she could not have her pony, or how the extra special birthday present she'd longed for was too expensive because the money had to go on Elinor instead.

Many children who grew up listening to such things would have come to hate the outsider they were forced to share their home with, but Sophie was not one of them. She adored Elinor thinking of her more as a big sister than a cousin, and was hurt when the teenager set people straight about their true relationship.

However, the real problem between Elinor and Max had nothing to do with money. It was much simpler, yet somehow more complicated than that. It was because the girl unnerved him, and he was not alone in his opinion that there was something strange about the girl who seemed to be followed around by death.

Some of the incidents could be explained away as mere coincidences. Taken individually, there was nothing striking about the events which occurred, but added together it was hard to ignore the wake of destruction Elinor left behind her.

Her birth parents had died in the car crash. Soon after she was taken in by Eve and Ben and on the day they brought the baby home, where the whole family had gathered to greet the new addition, death descended again. They placed the baby into the arms of their elderly grandmother who, having held the child for a few seconds complained of feeling unwell. Moments later she was dead.

When Elinor was two years old she had apparently babbled the words,

"Pup gone." Less than a minute later the pet dog escaped the garden and was killed by a passing car.

Whenever a death occurred, natural or otherwise, Elinor was nearby either at the time or shortly before, and she always seemed to have prior knowledge of its approach. She could watch a bird of prey in the sky and point out precisely where it would make its kill. She would give advance warning of birds about to fly headlong into the patio doors and instinctively knew when someone's time on earth was up. The worst incident though, and the one which frightened even the most sceptical of listeners, concerned her guardians.

The day began was like any other. Ben had gone to work and Eve was at home looking after Elinor. In the early afternoon, Eve remembered she needed some shopping picking up, and decided to call Ben and ask him to do it on his way home to save her having to travel to the other side of town.

"Let's call your daddy," she said to Elinor, walking to the phone.

"He won't answer," Elinor replied.

This statement would not have bothered most people, but coming from the child who seemed to have a natural affinity with death, the words froze Eve's blood. She said nothing but looked at the six year old, who stared at the clock, trance like, before saying,

"Bang, bang. He won't answer."

Eve hurried to the phone which was engaged. She dialled time and time again, but it went unanswered. Worried, she packed Elinor into the car and sped off across the town to the store where her husband worked.

Imediately, it was obvious something bad had happened. There were police everywhere, and the area around Ben's work place was cordoned off. Hysterical with fear, Eve demanded to know what had happened, and after causing a scene and screaming about her husband, they broke the news to her. There had been a robbery at the store and, at precisely the time Elinor had been staring at the clock, Ben had been shot and killed by one of the robbers.

Poor Eve. She had been so in love with Ben, it was too great a loss for her to bear.

The night of his funeral, leaving Elinor in the care of Sarah, Eve hanged herself from the staircase of their home. Again,

Elinor seemed to be aware of it even as it was happening. She would not settle at her aunt and uncle's house, and kept saying how her mummy was dying. No-one listened. They assumed she was afraid that having lost her father, her mother would disappear too. Sadly, Elinor was right and Sarah found the body of her step-sister the following morning.

Her predictions did not end there either, so maybe Max could be forgiven for thinking the girl he had been forced to take in was weird. Mind you, it was the only thing he could be forgiven for.

In addition to this, Elinor had several other curious strains to her nature. She had never been ill, not once. She had not suffered from so much as a sniffle in her life, and it went further still. Despite numerous accidents, some quite severe, she escaped without picking up the tiniest scratch. She appeared indestructible. The one weak spot in her otherwise impenetrable armour was as bizarre as the girl herself.

She had an almost pathological loathing for dolls houses. The mention of one was enough to turn the girl white with fear, but the sight of one reduced her to a nervous wreck. She had suffered from a recurring nightmare which involved an old toy house that was hidden away in a dingy room for so many years, that as frightening as the dream was, its regular occurrence it ceased to scare her. Why this most unlikely of items produced such fear, no-one ever knew and nobody felt the inclination to look into the causes behind it.

The problem was that at times it was hard for Elinor not to feel responsible for Sarah's and Sophie's hardships. Max had, in many ways, been right. If they had not had to pay out on stuff for her, the Cutter family would have had a lot more money to spend on themselves. Sarah did her best to set Elinor's mind at ease over such things (which she never really succeeded in doing), whenever the girl put this theory forward.

"Don't be foolish," she would say, "Max managed to find the money to take Miss impossibly-long-legs out to posh restaurants and for weekends in country hotels. He is the only person responsible for this mess, and maybe myself for not having seen what he was up to sooner."

Inside, the house felt as daunting as it had looked from the outside, and even with their hurried breathing and shuffling feet, a strange quiet seemed to permeate everything.

"I'm glad Frank and Rachel came over to tidy the place last weekend," Sarah said lowering her box to the ground. "I couldn't face having to organize a house at this moment in time."

Frank was Sarah's older brother, and Rachel his wife. They had no children of their own and doted on both girls. At the time of Eve and Ben's deaths, they wanted to have Elinor come live with them, but the company Frank worked for back then frequently sent him overseas, sometimes for months at a time and Rachel went wherever his job took him. They did not think such a lifestyle was right for raising a child in as there was no stability to it.

It had been less than three years since they moved back home permanently, which was when Frank set up his own law firm. Again, the pair offered to take Elinor in, but each time Sarah refused. She seemed convinced there was a reason she had been the one who ended up taking care of her. Elinor wished Sarah would allow her to move in with Frank and Rachel, not because she was ungrateful to Sarah, but because it might have made life easier for all concerned. Anyway, it was academic now.

"I'm going to make us a drink. Why don't you two go up and find your rooms? Frank said they picked ones they knew you'd like. Sophie, yours is on the next floor at the front, and Elinor yours is up in the attic."

"Great!" Elinor muttered under her breath, "Up in the servants quarters." Sarah, who had hearing a bat would be jealous of, heard the remark.

"Actually, your aunt and uncle thought you might appreciate a bit of privacy."

It turned out they had made the right choice. Sophie had been given a brightly painted room with nice white bedroom furniture that radiated with the very essence of cheerfulness, but the attic was much more to Elinor's taste.

The exposed wooden beams of the ceiling reached across the roof between walls that were painted a deep shade of purple, apart from the wall behind the headboard of her bed, which was exposed and made up of the same grey stone the house was built from. The furniture was much more in-keeping with the period the property too; everything was made of dark wood, except for the bed which was metal and gothic in style. The floor boards were covered by a large black rug which ended a few inches short of the skirting boards on each wall. Elinor liked it the instant she opened the door.

She dropped her bag at the foot of her bed, and looked around. For the first time in weeks she felt happy. From the squeals of glee coming from the floor below, it was obvious Sophie shared the sentiment.

"Look! Ponies in the field opposite. Can you see them too, Ellie?" Though she had two small windows which gazed out in the same direction Sophie's room faced, Elinor was drawn to the larger window that stood in another wall. "Can you see them, Ellie?"

"Yes," Elinor lied as she pulled back the thin net curtain hanging over her chosen view point.

The window, which was at the side of the house next to the neglected track, had no view as such. It was possible to see the road as it wound further on into the village, but for the most part, there was nothing other than the old stone wall with its even older trees to be seen. From her higher vantage point though, she had a good view of what their branches shielded.

Reaching on, scattered and apparently forgotten, was what looked to be an old graveyard. She assumed it was no longer in use, as, from what she could see, many of the once proud memorials were overgrown, broken or had collapsed entirely.

"Cool," Elinor whispered. "Should be able to get some good photos down there."

That was Elinor's ambition; to be a photographer, and luckily for her, the college in the nearby city ran a course in it. If they hadn't she would have been forced to choose between two options. The first was to give up on her dream career and find something else to do with her life. The second even less appealing choice was to have stayed put in her old home town and for Sarah and Sophie to have moved away without her. It wasn't that being alone bothered her. Elinor was quite at home with her own company, but not moving to Mournsby would have made life incredibly difficult for her aunt, who had quite enough to deal with.

Sarah depended on her so much, especially since the divorce, and despite appearances, the teenager was not so selfish as to pull a vanishing act precisely at the moment she was really needed. Doing so would have been more than a little ungrateful.

After unpacking their few belongings, which did not take much time, the housemates set about preparing their supper. It would have been easier to order a takeaway or go out for a meal, but as Elinor pointed out, by the time the delivery turned up, providing the driver could locate the house in the first place, it would be closer to breakfast than dinner. They also realized they had no idea as to where the nearest pub was as, unsurprisingly, Mournsby didn't have even that basic facility, so it would be far quicker to simply cook a meal for themselves.

With nearest supermarket being on the outskirts of the city, it was a good job Frank and Rachel had stocked the kitchen with every food they could find. In the end, they had baked potatoes with vegetable pies and treacle tart with custard for desert. It was not the most exciting of meals, but it was the most appreciated. It was amazing how hungry the move had made them.

Elinor took care of the washing up while Sarah gave her daughter a bath and put her to bed. Sophie kept saying she was not tired, but barely two pages in her bedtime story she was fast asleep. She was not the only one tired out by the day. Elinor was exhausted herself, and found it difficult to conceal her yawns as she flicked between the five TV stations available to locals. She had often wondered how people coped without cable or satellite, now she was going to find out.

"Why don't you go to bed, Elle?" Sarah said, still trying to arrange her ornaments in a way she liked. "You were up before all of us this morning, and didn't get in until late last night."

"I wanted to enjoy a final night of fun with my friends, being as we decided to move here right at the start of the summer holidays. Couldn't we have left it a few weeks? You don't start your new job for another fortnight." Sarah sighed.

"We had to vacate the flat when we did because the lease was up. I've told you this several times already. I'm sorry you feel hard done by, but this situation is no more to my liking than it is to yours."

A pang of guilt hit Elinor as she saw her aunt's face pained by the remembrance of shattered dreams.

"Sorry," she muttered.

"It's okay. Besides, it will give us a chance to get to know the area better before we plunge into a new life here." Elinor snorted dismissively.

"Based on the journey, that should take us a spectacular three minutes ten seconds!" Sarah gave a small grin as she saw there was no malice intended in her niece's words.

"Oh, talk sense. That's the time needed to reach the far end of the village. You neglected to add on the three minutes ten seconds it will take to get back to house." Elinor smiled too.

"Sorry. My mistake. I think I will go up actually. Who knows, maybe the additional height will enable me to get a signal on my mobile. I'd like to let my friends know I arrived on Planet Nowhere safe and well."

In her room, Elinor tried, without success, to get a signal on her phone. It made no difference where she stood or in what position she twisted her body, the phone refused to accept there was a world beyond the four walls of the house.

Having almost fallen off her bed for the third time, Elinor conceded defeat, and decided to go to call it a night. She felt drained and knew the next few days were going to be manic. The house still needed sorting, they had to locate the shops and find their way around the village. She drew the curtains of the windows overlooking the front of the house, but when she went to do the same with the side one, something outside caught her attention, something that made Elinor wonder if she had gone mad.

Across the road, beyond the wall and the trees she could have sworn there were lights floating about in mid-air over in the cemetery. Thinking her eyes were playing tricks on her, she blinked hard, and looked again. She was relieved to begin with, for there was nothing to be seen, but as she was about to turn away they reappeared, and this time there were more of them.

Elinor stood motionless as the lights, which looked to be about the size of a tennis ball, weaved and crossed their way between the graves, illuminating each stone for a brief moment as it passed by. She laughed at the thought, even as it entered her mind, but to her it seemed as if they were searching for something. As they moved into the distance and out of her view, she shook her head in bemusement.

"Weird. Definitely weird." She turned off the lights and climbed into bed and let out a long sigh. Almost at once, she was asleep.

But the strange goings on were not so easy to escape as that. She had been plagued by strange dream about a toy house for as long as she could remember, but the one which visited her that night, was entirely different. She was stood on the street of the village directly outside a set of huge old metal gates set into a stone wall similar to the one she could see from her room that marked the edge of the cemetery. It was twilight, and a cold wind blew fiercely as night approached, wrapping itself around her as it headed into the village.

Elinor followed it, but she was apparently not alone. Barely more than a whisper, and carried on the wind she heard a voice coming from everywhere and no-where, that was both quite but deafening at the same time which echoed about her as she walked.

> "A grey shroud of sorrow, of loss and of pain,
> Shall cover the village bearing grief's name,
> Unending,
> Unbroken,
> The innocent cries shall silent remain,
> Until deaths grace returns there again."

The wind picked up, causing the rusty barrier to shake violently as they battled against the chain which bound them, as if something invisible was trying to break free. Elinor began to reach her hand out towards them, an act which only increased the intensity with which the gates shook, as the voice continued.

"The gates they will part,
A beginning to the end of shadow and dark."

A crack reverberated throughout the now pitch black sky with such intensity, it sounded as if the earth itself had split open, and the lock which fastened the chain restraining the wildly vibrating gates, shattered and the chain dropped to the ground.

Elinor jerked bolt upright with a gasp. Her eyes flicked wildly around as she tried to work out where she was. Her pulse eased once she was able to make out the shape of a wardrobe on the far side of the room, and she realized she was in the safety of the house. She flopped back down into bed and took a deep breath to calm her nerves. Mournsby was not going to be as relaxing as she thought it would be.

Chapter Four

A New Mystery

The next morning Elinor, who was usually the first person up, rose shortly after dawn. It was then she discovered two disadvantages to having a bedroom in the attic of an old house. The first was the number of squeaky floor boards she had to negotiate her way around. The second was that being on the top most floor of the house meant there was further to travel in order to reach the front door. The combination of the two virtually guaranteed to alert her aunt or cousin to her movements. Fortunately, both were heavy sleepers, so despite the variety of creaks, groans and squeaks that answered each carefully taken footstep, she reached the front garden without having disturbed anyone.

Elinor took a deep breath of the cool morning air to refresh her weary brain. The sky was a soft shade of orange as the sun emerged from below the horizon. Apart from the birds singing in the hedgerows, the distant bleat of a sheep and the occasional rustle from the trees as the breeze danced through their branches, it was perfectly silent. It was as if the world had been reborn during the hours of darkness, and lay there before her, crisp, and clean and full of promise. Had she been living in the city, there would have been few people out and about at such an early hour. In Mournsby there was no-one at all. She could have been the last person on the planet.

This lack of company allowed Elinor to drop the façade of contentment she presented to the world, so she could be herself. Normally, she felt as if she was acting out a part.

People expected her to be someone she wasn't and behave in some expected but unspecified manner. It was in these rare moments she could allow her mind to wander aimlessly through a thousand questions and imaginings which cascaded into her mind, without having to worry what the person next to her was thinking or saying.

She strolled off down the garden path and away from the house. Usually her wanderings were not planned. She typically walked and thought until she had had enough which was when she returned home. Today was different. She had a specific place she wanted to seek out. The combined effects of the lights in the graveyard and her dream had kept her up most of the night. She had mused over them for hours on end, yet could not make sense of what either might have meant, but she was determined to find out.

The all-encompassing wall was far too high for her to see over, except from her window of course, and climbing up it seemed equally impossible, so she began to search for the main entrance. Whether or not her dream was accurate, there had to be one, despite the site not having been used for some time.

The wall separating the graveyard from the village street continued on, with only a few sections having succumbed to time, but still it remained too high for Elinor to see beyond as if determined to keep its secrets locked away from prying eyes. Finally she found it. Lost behind years of wild undergrowth was the gateway which led to where generations of Mournsby's residents had been laid to rest. At least the teenager hoped they were at rest.

The gate was no more welcoming than the walls. She could not help noting they were the same as the ones in her dream, which was unnerving enough, but it was more than that which caused a thrill of dread to sweep through her.

Standing there before the rusty barriers that towered high into the air, Elinor detected an atmosphere of foreboding coming from the other side. It was so oppressive anyone less determined would have quickly turned on their heels and run in the opposite direction.

However, feelings of despair did not bother the girl in the slightest. She had, after all, been in their company most of her life. So rather than fleeing back towards the bright glow of dawn, which covered the lands behind her, she edged closer to the overcast grounds.

She pushed through the thorny brambles, which stabbed at her jeans as if trying to stop her from moving forward, until, scratched and bleeding, Elinor was stood with her face inches away from the metal bars which stood between her and the land beyond.

There was very little to see as it happened. This was due, in part she assumed, because the sun, although bathing the rest of the village in a sea of light, had not reached the cemetery, leaving it cloaked in a grey shroud that seemed to be impenetrable. The cause for this was most likely to it being surrounded by high walls and tall trees, but that did not make the contrast between the two sides of the village any less alarming. Another reason for her lack of clear sight was, like the verge outside its walls, the cemetery was lost beneath a veritable jungle of weeds and plant life of every type imaginable who had claimed the burial plots for their own.

Watching in silence, Elinor carefully examined the forgotten place, occasionally picking out the head of an angelic statue or the tip of a cross which marked the spot where someone once held dear, now lay remembered by none. It was silly, but Elinor thought how sad a spot it seemed. Of course, graveyards were not known for their limitless laughter, but it wasn't a sadness caused by the memory of so many people having passed from this world and the loved ones left behind to mourn them she could detect. Such despair would be tinged with age. What Elinor could pick up was fresh, deep and painful. A sorrow so intense it reached, not only far back into the past, but out into the future, unless…

"Unless what you idiot?!" She scolded herself sharply. "Pull yourself together girl. This place is bound to have a deep seated air of depression. It is centuries old, there are probably hundreds of people buried there, which means thousands of mourners would have traipsed through here at some point. It's hardly going to feel like a holiday camp!"

A blackbird cried in alarm from the field behind her, causing Elinor to break free from her wonderings. She looked down at the chain and padlock which kept the gates bound tightly shut to the outside world. They were coated in a thick layer of rust. No-one had passed through them in many a moon. So, what were the lights she had seen in the supposedly locked cemetery the night before?

"You dreamt it," she said, trying to convince herself everything was normal. "By the look of this lock, this is the closest anyone living has been to this place since before Queen Victoria was born."

Yet, even as she spoke and began to turn away, Elinor's sharp eyes spotted something which clearly disproved her theory. Some distance beyond the entrance, hiding behind a few weed encased headstones was a narrow, well-trodden pathway. It was impossible from her position to see where it began or led to, but elsewhere not so much as a blade of grass had been disturbed, which made the small, winding track-way that headed off into the deeper parts of the cemetery, stand out all the more.

There was but one explanation for this; someone or something walked that route with regularity. Elinor shuddered and began to move off towards the road. Apart from the fact her aunt would soon be up, and if she found Elinor to be missing would assume the girl had run back to her friends, she did not like the way the gloom of the cemetery seemed to be honing in on her.

Elinor forced her way back to the pavement, and with one last glance at the gates, headed back in the direction of the house. The closer she got to home, the more the sorrow she had picked up on eased, and the happier she became, but still she could not shake off the feeling that something had attached itself to her the moment she arrived in Mournsby, and it's fixation with her had intensified with her visit to the cemetery. Several times she checked over her shoulder, half convinced some unspeakable demon was trailing in her footsteps, but naturally there was nothing there. Also, rather than finding out the answers to the questions she had lain awake thinking about, she had instead landed herself with further riddles to solve. What were the lights she had seen floating about? What did her dream mean? Who had been walking in the seemingly locked and barred graveyard?

She reached the front door without realizing it, and let herself in. As she entered the hallway, the alarm clock in her aunt's room began to beep urgently. Elinor shut the door behind her, quietly but quickly so as to shut out whatever it was that followed her, though feeling that any such action was pointless for the damage was already done.

Chapter Five

New Discoveries, New Friends

Not only did Elinor make it back before her aunt was up, she also managed to get the kettle boiling and set the table for breakfast before Sarah made it downstairs.

"You're up early," Sarah yawned as her niece plugged in the toaster.

"No more than usual."

"Anything of interest to report?" Elinor thought about her experiences during the night and of her early morning trip to the village graveyard, the atmosphere of which still lingered about her. However, as people, her aunt included, thought Elinor odd enough, she guessed announcing the first place she had gone to visit was the local burial ground would be unlikely to go down well. She had to think quickly, as any delay in answering would be equally suspicious.

On the off chance Sarah had heard the door either opening or closing as Elinor went about her activities, the teenager said,

"Not so far. I waited on the steps with my camera for the sun to come up so I could get a few pictures." The lack of interest shown by her aunt meant she had slept through the pre-dawn comings and goings, and satisfied her story had been believed, Elinor set about making some breakfast.

Before long, Sophie joined the gathering in the kitchen, chattering away almost without pausing for breath. As the din around her increased, Elinor found herself wishing she was back at the cemetery, isolated and lost in the silence not even a song bird dared to disturb, a desire which puzzled her immensely.

She often longed to be away from the bustle of family life, especially as it was not really her family, but normally when she sought sanctuary at the house of one of her friends or went for a walk somewhere no-one who knew her was likely to be. This was different. She had no wish to be in contact with any person, at least not those who were living. Despite having returned with a feeling of oppression after her visit there, Elinor could not ignore a deep yearning to return to the cemetery, as if something was calling her back to the gates that marked the boundary between two worlds.

So lost in these thoughts did the teenager become, she forgot about the racket going on around her.

"Elinor!" The loud, not to mention noticeably sharp tone of her aunt's voice brought the girl out of her thoughts and back into the kitchen. The commotion had subsided and based on the expressions of Sarah and Sophie, it was immediately obvious several attempts had been made to attract her attention before it registered with the girl.

"Sorry. I was thinking."

"So it would seem. I asked if you had any plans for today." This was one of those questions which came with a silently implied part to it. Harmless a request as it sounded, Elinor knew 'do you have any plans?' actually meant, 'I hope you don't have anything planned for the day because I need you to do something for me.'

Usually in these situations, she had a ready to use excuse prepared to get out of any such unwelcome interruption to her schedule, but for the first time in years, Elinor was caught off guard. Apart from half of her usual reasons for not being free having been rendered null and void by the move to Mournsby, she had been so preoccupied with the questions raised by her morning investigations, her mind was swimming with images of eerie lights and gothic angels guarding the cemetery like watchers from another realm when the question came, they rendered her incapable of thinking up an excuse to get her out of whatever it was her aunt was about to drop on her.

"I take it from your silence that would be a 'no' to my question?"

Defeated, Elinor said it was.

"Good. Then I have a favour to ask. Could you look after Sophie for a couple of hours? Take her out to explore the village or something. I've got a lot of stuff here to sort out and it will be much easier without the two of you interrupting me every other minute."

"A couple of hours?!" Elinor sighed in exasperation. A look of annoyance flashed over Sarah's face.

"Surely it's not too much to ask?"

"No," Elinor lied, "I'm just wondering what the hell there is to do out here that will take two hours. It's hardly an entertainment hotspot." The stare of annoyance changed to one of severe irritation, telling Elinor the subject was not actually up for discussion, so she went back to eating her toast.

Once breakfast was finished and Sophie had chosen which of her multitude of outfits she was going to wear, the cousins set out to explore Mournsby. For reasons unknown to her, Elinor's craving for the cemetery vanished when she contemplated going there with Sophie. Some sort of presentiment warned her against any such action, and trusting in her instincts, Elinor was determined to keep the young girl as far away from the place which had easily permeated her own mind as she possibly could. So, she took an entirely different route away from the house.

As expected, there was little to see in the village itself. It was mostly made up of houses, cottages and farm outbuildings, but as they left one of the so-called main roads, they came across something that showed they were not as cut off from the modern world as first appeared.

Tucked away behind rows of picturesque country cottages was the village green, and at its far end was a post office and general store, along with the ruin of the old church, which, from the information board set up for tourists on walking holidays, had inexplicably caught fire in the early 1900s. Sophie was fascinated, particularly by the old red telephone box that stood at the edge of the green. She had never seen one before, and thought them much better than the modern ones. Elinor agreed entirely.

The store, which was run by Mr and Mrs Braxton, the owners of the house Elinor and her family were renting, were initially confused by the appearance of two youngsters. It took Mrs Braxton a few minutes to recollect their meeting the day before, but as soon as she did, the husband and wife were more than welcoming.

"It has been many a long year since we've had children living in Mournsby, never mind two such delightful angels as yourselves. It's mostly elderly or retired folks out here, all desperate to escape the hectic pace of the modern world."

"I'll have to look at modernizing my stock if there are going to be children coming in with regularity," Mr Braxton, or Fred, as his wife called him, added. "How long has it been since we had any youngsters here?"

What happened next only served to puzzle Elinor further. Neither Frank nor Bess Braxton could recall how long it had been since anyone under the age of fifty had resided in the village. Their minds were a complete blank.

This memory lapse was not restricted to the store's owners. Four other customers came in while Elinor and Sophie were there, and they were equally clueless. Not sure if the wide spread forgetfulness was due to there being something in the water or because they had been out in the sticks for so long they'd all gone barmy, Elinor bought some sweets for her cousin, handed over the shopping list her aunt had presented her with before leaving the house, then made a swift exit from the shop.

They had barely gone two steps, when a voice called out loudly, and there was no mistaking it was a remark aimed at the two girls.

"Blimey! Look. There are people under the age of a hundred out here. I thought we were going to be condemned to a summer of knitting patterns and lectures on how to drive moles from the garden!" Elinor and Sophie turned around to see a boy and girl, about Elinor's age, approaching across the green.

"Do you know them?" Sophie asked, with her mouth full of sweets.

"Not yet."

"Glad to see there's someone in this place who doesn't believe creases in your jeans are the height of fashion," the boy added as he and his companion joined the cousins. Elinor laughed.

"They probably knew at one point, but with how absent minded people are here, it's probably slipped their minds!"

"You've noticed that too, have you?" the girl said in answer to Elinor's joke. "Our grandparents used to be as sharp as a box of knives, but since they moved here, they struggle to remember our names. Which reminds me, time for an introduction, I think. I'm Emma. Well, Em, and the loud hailer beside me is my brother, Rick."

"Elinor, and this is Sophie." Sophie had to wave in acknowledgement as she was in the process of swallowing her sweets.

"Hi. She is so cute," Emma cooed. "I sometimes wish I had a sister, instead of this great lug."

"She's not…" Elinor began to say, but in an unexpectedly sarcastic voice, Sophie cut her off, finishing the sentence herself.

"Not actually my sister."

Having reduced the gathering to silence, Sophie shrugged her shoulders, and wandered off to where one of the village cats was sunning itself on the warm tarmac.

"Sorry about her," Elinor apologized. "It's a complicated situation, our family life." Rick and Emma decided not to enquire further seeing as they had only just met. Prying into someone's family life when, by their own admission, it was complicated, would have been nothing short of tactless.

"Well, as we seem to be the only four people within a hundred miles who were not alive when this place was actually built, perhaps you can show us around?" Rick said. "We've never been here before, you see. Our grandparents, whom we spend every summer with, while our parents go off exploring some distant part of the globe, used to live in the city, but they retired here a few months back."

"Ah, sorry I can't help you either. We moved her ourselves only yesterday. It was by luck rather than judgement we found the shop."

"Maybe it wasn't luck either," Emma said mysteriously. "Maybe something led you here."

Having already been confronted by Mournsby's other-worldly atmosphere, the remark registered more strongly with Elinor than it usually would have.

"Ignore my sister. It's not the country air affecting her behaviour, she's always been weird."

"Just because I happen to think there's more to this world than what we can see." Rick rolled his eyes.

"Trust me to wind up with a weirdy for a sister. At least with you about I'll have someone normal to talk to when she nips off to Planet Supernatural." Elinor gave Rick a mocking smile.

"Sorry to disappoint you, but I'm a confirmed resident of said planet myself." Emma and Elinor gave each other a high five as Rick gave an exaggerated groan.

"That's it then. I am officially the last sane person left in this village. Mind you, if I spend too much time here I doubt that will be the case for long."

The three teenagers collected Sophie and decided to explore Mournsby together. They swapped tales about their lives, although Elinor was reluctant to go into her past in too much detail. She was embarrassed by it, but because it had a tendency to depress people she thought the less she talked about it, the better. Sophie was not bound by such emotions. Rick and Emma had already guessed their family life was far from straight forward, but didn't want to appear nosey. When Rick had explained his parent's obsession with adventure holidays probably being something to do with the boring jobs they did, Emma asked what Elinor's mother and father did. Before she could reply, her young cousin blurted out,

"Nothing. They're all dead."

An awkward pause hung in the air between the new friends.

"Sorry," Emma finally mumbled. "It can't be easy losing both parents." Sophie though, had not finished making waves.

"She's not lost both her parents. She's lost all four of them." Again, the quiet air of speechlessness descended. Thanks to her cousin's lack of tact, Elinor was forced to reveal the truth about her skill for losing guardians. She did not go into too much detail, and thankfully when she told them about her aunt's divorce, not even Sophie blurted out how Max thought Elinor was the Angel of Death in disguise.

Without following a specific route, the four strolled on around the village, and thankfully, the conversation switched back to more cheerful subjects. They chatted on about everything and nothing, or at least Elinor, Rick and Emma did. Sophie, being that much younger, could not understand half of the stuff they were talking about. To her, it was complete nonsense and as they walked, realizing she had little to offer the conversation, she sped up, until she was a good hundred yards ahead of the noisy trio, who seemed to be oblivious to her presence.

That changed as Elinor caught a glimpse of a familiar sight. It was the old stone wall of the cemetery, and it was on the opposite side of the road to where they were. Though the sun was shining, Elinor went cold as it dawned on her they must have come round full circle during their walk, and now were on the only available path to be seen. Elinor muttered a silent reprimand to herself for leading Sophie to the one spot in Mournsby she had been determined to keep her away from. Her sudden exit from the conversation might have been noticed, had it not been for the fact that at the very same moment she fell quiet, her companions also stopped speaking.

Their attention was entirely focused on Sophie, who was no longer on the path ahead of them. She had crossed the road and was stood at the edge of a driveway, which disappeared from sight as it twisted through the trees growing along its length. The point where the driveway joined the road was the only spot where the otherwise impenetrable wall was broken, and Sophie was mesmerized by it.

"Sophie!" Elinor shouted sounding angrier than she meant to. She hurried over to her cousin when she did not respond to her call, and spun the girl around by her shoulders. Her anger gave way to concern as she beheld the glazed expression on the child's face, which faded as Elinor's arrival shattered whatever charm had led Sophie there, leaving the child confused as to how she came to be there.

"You know better than to cross a road on your own."

"I'm sorry. I didn't mean too. I can't remember crossing it at all." Rick and Emma said nothing about the mini squabble which was over as soon as it had started.

"I think it is best I get you back home," Elinor sighed, still worried by Sophie's strange behaviour.

The friends continued on together so that Elinor could show Rick and Emma where her house was, but they said little more on the way. Elinor took a sideways glance at the cemetery gates as they passed them, which held her attention in the same way the driveway had captivated her cousin, and quite accidentally revealing yet another riddle to be unravelled.

The driveway was a ridiculously short distance away from the very spot where Elinor had stood earlier in the day, yet then there had been no sign of it. The verge had been unbroken in both directions as far as they eye could see. There was no path or walkway, let alone a gravelled drive. She may have been spooked but her senses had not been disturbed enough to have missed something as obvious as a thundering great gap in the very obstacle she had been trying to climb over. She had somehow stumbled into something strange that day, and Elinor had the horrid feeling it was the first of many more instances still to come.

Chapter Six

Welcome Home

The rest of the day passed slowly and without incident. Sarah wondered if the two girls had fallen out again they were so quiet, but as each denied the accusation when questioned separately, she put their lack of communication down to tiredness and decided to leave well alone.

What Sophie was thinking, Elinor could hardly guess, mainly because her own head was so full of puzzles, and, so as not to add to the already vast pile of questions she had to find the answers to she left Sophie to her own devices.

Sitting in the shade of the willow tree which grew at the far end of the garden to the rear of the house, Elinor did her best to reason things out, with no success. She tried to rationalize her fears. The whole thing about the cemetery being eerie was quite natural. Countless people were buried there and no-one had entered the place for decades, so it was going to have an air of abandonment about it. To her, that sounded like a well-reasoned explanation. The trouble was there was a flaw to her theory. The single frequently walked route cutting through the otherwise undisturbed weeds. Someone had been inside the cemetery walls recently, and trod the same path time and time again.

Then there were the bizarre lights to consider. Elinor had heard tales of orbs similar to those she'd seen being spotted in similar sites, and these had been put down to gases escaping from newly interred bodies. Her lights could not have been caused by such a phenomenon. They were too small, too quick and roamed freely throughout the graveyard. Not even a strong wind could cause gas to move at such high speeds. Besides, as years had gone by since anyone had been buried there such vapours would have ceased being produced long ago. (She quickly dismissed the idea of a more recent, secret burial having occurred. The situation was complicated enough without suspecting that someone in the village was a murderer.)

So, Elinor could not explain away the strange effect the cemetery had on her, which in turn prevented her from finding a way to convince herself that, thanks to her overactive imagination, she had simply missed the driveway which magically appeared during their walk.

Still her doubts lingered. Could she really have been so frightened her usually observant brain had shut down temporarily? No, it was unlikely. She had been caught up in far more risky situations in the past and retained control of her mind, which led her to conclude the driveway was not present when she went for her early morning trek. So how was it possible for it to appear there a few hours later?

It was a fruitless exercise. She was going round in circles. Elinor shook her head in an attempt to free it of such crazy ideas, but as the day wore on, each discarded thought squirmed its way back into her mind.

By supper time, Sophie had snapped out of her subdued mood, and apparently had no recollection of what happened after they had left the store. Sarah was happy to discover there were a couple of other youngsters in Mournsby. She had been sure one morning she would come down to breakfast to find her determined niece had headed back to the friends she'd left behind. She hoped having people her own age living a few streets away would help Elinor settle into her new life that bit quicker.

Once Sophie had gone to bed, Elinor sat with her aunt watching the television as usual, but she was not really concentrating on the programme. She felt more exhausted than she had the night before, and remembered how little sleep she'd had, but worried that going to bed early for the second night in a row, especially after being so quiet throughout the afternoon would appear anti-social, and so she determined to stick it out for as long as possible.

It was a great relief when the phone rang, and it turned out to be her uncle on the other end of the line. Sarah would be busy talking to her brother for hours, so Elinor took advantage of the interruption and headed up to her room. She edged passed Sophie's door and dragged herself up to the attic.

Without taking so much as a brief glance out of a window she dropped down onto her bed. She wanted a night of unbroken sleep, and going light spotting would just bring her concerns about the goings-on in the graveyard to mind once more. She pushed her head into the cool, soft pillows and before she knew it, Elinor was fast asleep.

Sleep may have come quickly, but it was not peaceful. Once the house was shrouded in darkness, and those within were lost in dreams, outside the house something stirred softly on the breeze.

From the deepest recesses of the cemetery two small balls of pulsating light whipped between the headstones until they neared the wall marking the boundary of their world, but this did not stop them. On they flew and up, over the stone structure, across the track-way and towards the house closest to them.

The orbs came to a halt, hovering outside the closed window as they seemingly peered into the room beyond, casting weird patterns over the teenage girl who lay on the bed beyond the thin sheet of glass which separated them.

The visitors resumed their flying, climbing higher into the sky until they reached the chimney top. Without hesitation they dropped down into it, emerging in the very room the girl was sleeping in. Coming to rest at the foot of her bed, the lights flashed brilliantly, filling the room as their intensity increased. Elinor stirred slightly as the flickering subsided and the room was illuminated with a pale, candle-like glow.

"Elinor," a gentle, yet unnatural voice called out. "Elinor, be brave. You are not alone. Elinor."

The agitation she felt grew stronger as from out of the light, a hand, which had no more substance to it than a cobweb did, reached out towards her, it's white skin appearing all the more lifeless due to the brightly shining ruby red stone that was set into the golden ring it wore. As it approached, a cold draught ran across Elinor's body, following the hand's movement precisely as it stretched its fingers towards her face. The spirit had her almost within its grasp, when alerted by some instinct that warned of the invaders, Elinor woke in terror.

The room was in complete darkness and she was alone. Elinor tried to calm herself as she wiped away the cold sweat that had broken out on her forehead. Nothing appeared to have been disturbed. Everything was exactly as it had been when she went to bed, although she did notice the temperature had dropped considerably.

Elinor turned on the lamp beside her bed and lay down. It was hardly surprising she was having nightmares about disembodied spirits. She had been obsessed by thoughts of dead people and graveyards all day, hardly conducive to a good night's rest.

Although the adrenaline was still running through her body, Elinor rolled onto her side, determined to settle down and go back to sleep, which was when she saw it. In the darkness of the room she had overlooked the one change to have taken place following her dream.

On the desk, where her notebooks, pens and papers were stacked, she noticed the top book was wide open, and on the floor directly below the desk was a pen. Elinor's breath caught in her lungs. She was compulsively tidy and had left the books shut, with the pen sat in its holder when she last used them. Ignoring every impulse to remain precisely where she was until daylight returned, Elinor forced her legs to work, and finding it hard not to run away with fear, she crossed over to the desk.

Her legs buckled, and she almost dropped to the floor as her eyes locked onto the exposed page before her. In writing so broken and disjointed it looked as if it had been written by someone who had never used a pen before, were two words scribbled into the paper.

'Welcome back.'

Elinor had to clasp her hand over her mouth to prevent the cry that rose from her lungs from taking to the air. She wanted to run out of the room, but her body refused to move. She was at a loss as to how she should act because all her mind could do was focus on those words. She might be able to put the lights and her dreams down as being products of a wild imagination or sleepless nights, but this?

Unable to flee, Elinor had to use the desk to keep herself upright for she found it impossible to move even the short distance back to where her bed was, which was just as well. For had she made that short journey, which would have led her past the window from which she witnessed the events that first brought about her problems, she would have seen two balls of light racing away from her window and disappearing back into the gloom amid the gravestones from where they had come.

Chapter Seven
Mrs Barrowhyde

To Elinor's relief, the next few days were considerably quieter. Though her unexpected greeting in the middle of the night had left her frightened and, once again, short on sleep, when daylight returned, things seemed much better.

Upon re-examining her notebook and the poorly written words left in it, Elinor thought how childish they looked, and concluded Sophie, in some pathetic attempt to scare her, had gone up to the attic while Elinor and Sarah were downstairs and left the message there for her to find at some later point. After all, Elinor had not taken the time to look around the room when she went to bed; she had simply flopped down and gone to sleep. As for her dreams, well, she still thought her original idea was the right one. Having spent an entire day focusing on death, she had naturally gone on to dream about it. Problems solved!

Rick and Emma became regular visitors to the house, and were as overjoyed as Elinor was to have someone their own age to hang around with. What time they did not spend at End Cottage was divided up between rambling about the village and going to Rick and Emma's grandparent's home, which was tucked away at the very back end of Mournsby.

It was a much older property than the one Elinor and Sophie lived in, and had a huge garden, which was not far off being the size of a small field. Emma and Rick's grandparents, Mr and Mrs Haskell, were nice enough people and were clever enough to realize their presence was not always required let alone wanted when the teenagers got together, but as the house and it's grounds were on the large side, it was quite easy keeping out of one another's way.

At least it was once the grown-ups remembered why there were children roaming about their property. Elinor and Sophie might have been regular callers, but each time they knocked on the Haskell's door, Elinor had to explain who she was and why she was calling to whoever answered it and the recurring memory loss was not confined only to her friend's grandparents.

Indeed, the whole of Mournsby, or rather those residents of the village they had met on more than one occasion, appeared to be afflicted with the same absent minded condition. Each time they went to the shop or bumped into someone familiar to them, Elinor had to re-introduce herself all over again. It was not only bizarre, it was incredibly irritating.

Elinor found herself being left in charge of Sophie on a regular basis too over those days. Aunt Sarah was busy in the city, making sure she was ready to start her new job, and was having to spend her final few days of unemployment sorting out her works identification pass and car parking permit. To say she felt put upon was an understatement, but Elinor quickly decided against saying anything following a most unexpected, not to mention unwelcome, phone call from Sarah's ex-husband, which put her into a bad mood like no other. It appeared everyone in the house was going to have to get on with things however unpleasant they might be.

With Sophie in her care, Elinor did her best to keep away from the cemetery. With her own bedroom looking out over its grounds, it was impossible for her not to catch sight of it at least once a day, and each time she did, the more she became convinced it was not the place of eternal rest it made itself out to be. It was a place where evil lurked, an evil that was forever on the watch, waiting to strike.

Seeing the lights flitting about the headstones on a nightly basis did nothing to ease these fears, but the thing that worried her most was how the more she tried to ignore the place, the deeper her fascination with it became. Each morning before her family were up, Elinor left the house and made her way to the gates which prevented her from disturbing the secrets it held.

The graveyard continued to haunt, not just her daylight wonderings, but her evening ones as well. Every night the dream would return in which she, pulled on by an unseen hand, drifted through the village to those very same gates, accompanied by the ghostly voice that repeated the rhyme she had heard on her first night in Mournsby.

"A grey shroud of sorrow, of loss and of pain,
Shall cover the village bearing grief's name.
Unending,
Unbroken,
The innocent cries shall silent remain,
Until deaths grace returns there again.
With a touch of a hand,
The gates they will part,
A beginning to the end of shadow and dark."

Each time Elinor would wake with a start because she knew there was more to come. That voice had more to tell her, this she was sure of for it followed her everywhere. She often fancied she had heard whispers, voices calling to her on the evening breeze as she stood in the garden or sat by an open window. Determined as she was to minimize her contact with the cemetery it seemed Fate had other ideas for time after time she was lured back to that one spot. The question was, why?

About a week after their arrival, another curious incident occurred, though Elinor instinctively recognized it was connected to those she was already mixed up in.

It was a glorious summer's day, and Elinor, Sophie, Rick and Emma were making the most of it by hiking around Mournsby's many tracks and bridleways that weaved across the countryside.

They had not been planning on going anywhere as it happened, but when the Haskells announced they were holding a barbecue for their friends in the village, Emma suggested they escaped as soon as possible. The idea of having their cheeks pinched and squeezed by countless pensioners as they remarked on how cute they were held no appeal, not even to Sophie who adored being the centre of attention. So, along with the Haskell's dog, Billy, the foursome headed off to find sanctuary in the fields.

The day was the best one of summer so far. Elinor did not find herself constantly thinking about dead people, Sophie, who had been unusually restrained since discovering the mysterious driveway, was darting about like a demented pixie and would not stop talking. Rick and Emma were also more outgoing, but it was too good to last. Mournsby's atmosphere of depression could not be so easily dispersed.

Without warning, Billy gave a loud bark and shot off with such speed he pulled poor Sophie clean off her feet, tearing his lead from her hand in the process. The dog refused to acknowledge the irate voices ordering him to stop and he continued to chase whatever it was that had captured his attention, and in seconds he was nothing more than a tiny blip on the horizon.

"Bloody dog," Rick cursed. "I bet he's after a rabbit. It's the one thing he can't resist having a go at. Sophie, are you okay?" She was fine because it was not just the wayward dog vanishing into the distance. Sophie, who bounced to her feet as if she was made of rubber, was likewise rapidly disappearing from view as she made after the dog, afraid of what might happen if Billy was involved in an accident. Ignoring her cut knees, she was up and off before anyone could utter a word of protest.

"Great!" Elinor declared with annoyance as her cried to wait went unheeded. "Now we have two run-aways to catch."

The three of them immediately joined the chase, which was beginning to look like a scene out of a comedy sketch show, when the comedy gave way to dismay as Elinor saw she had again been led back to the street which seemed to be stalking her. She was relieved however to see, a short distance away, Sophie and the dog had come to a halt, and they had company.

With the fugitive dog in her possession, Sophie was waiting at the edge of the very same driveway Elinor was sure had appeared after her initial visit to the cemetery, and with her was an elderly woman, dressed head to toe in black, old fashioned clothing. There was nothing extraordinary about the scene, yet something she could not put her finger on was wrong, and icy fingers up her spine advised her to be on guard.

Sophie and the old woman were so deep in conversation with one another neither of them paid attention to the approaching teenagers.

"Sophie! Do not run off like that. My life would not be worth living if I had to go home and say you'd gone missing," Elinor scolded before turning to the woman. "I'm sorry if she's caused you any bother," she said in her most apologetic tone. The old woman was obviously taken aback when the older girl addressed her, and it took a few moments for her to recover before answering.

"It's quite all right, my dear. The darling child has been no trouble whatsoever. I happened to see her passing by, and wondered what such a young thing was doing out here unaccompanied."

Her words were perfectly friendly but they were rendered meaningless by the rather cold stare the woman gave her. The rest of her appearance was equally out of place. The woman stood no more than five foot tall at best, and her head was crowned by grey, thinning hair, which she had pulled pack tightly into a bun. She was painfully thin, to the point where her razor sharp cheekbones protruded from under her aged skin.

It was a blazing hot afternoon, yet she wore a thick, black corded coat, which made her look even thinner. It had to be at least two sizes too big for her, and reached down to her ankles right from up underneath her chin, and every last button was fastened shut. She had on matching leather gloves so, with the exception of her face all that could be seen were the tips of her boots. She must have been boiling hot, but she looked as cold as winter.

"Well, thank you all the same. We'd best be getting home. Once again, sorry for the inconvenience, Mrs… Sorry, I don't know your name." The elderly lady smiled.

"Mrs Barrowhyde. I do hope I shall see you again soon," she said, brushing a stray piece of hair back behind Sophie's ear. "I love having children about the place. It's been too long since there were any here in the village." The words sent another wave of coldness through Elinor's blood, as if some terrible fate had just been decreed.

Trying to ignore the alarm bells clanging away in her ears, Elinor continued to be pleasant to their newest acquaintance, which was made more difficult by Mrs Barrowhyde herself. Although outwardly she was very welcoming, Mrs Barrowhyde viewed Elinor, Rick and Emma with unmasked suspicion. She eyed them nervously, as if something about their presence worried her. Sophie on the other hand received nothing but admiring stares of delight.

It could simply have been that, like many elderly people, Mrs Barrowhyde did not trust teenagers, and believed their arrival in Mournsby would shatter the peace of her quite little village. Based on their raucous arrival on her driveway, she could be forgiven for thinking that, but Elinor was far from convinced by her own argument. The way Mrs Barrowhyde constantly flicked her eyes from Elinor to Rick to Emma and back again suggested she was searching for something. Something so obscure it was hard to see, which increased the woman's paranoia further.

The village clock chimed the hour, bringing an end to Elinor's puzzling and the old lady's staring.

"We'd better be going," Rick sighed. "We promised to be back in time to say good bye to gran's guests. Nice to meet you Mrs Barrowhyde." Rick extended his hand as he bid farewell to the lady on behalf of himself and the others, but she did not accept or return the gesture.

"And you," she replied, her eyes locked onto Sophie with such intent it was clear she was not speaking to the entire group. Each comment made was aimed directly at the little girl. "Do feel free to pop in at any time. I have a large garden full of trees, swings and playhouses which are sadly no longer used since my children have moved into a house of their own."

Elinor was becoming nervous, and began to push her cousin in the direction of their own home. "It's very kind of you, but with getting ready for school and college, not to mention finishing the unpacking, I doubt we'll have the time spare." Finally, Mrs Barrowhyde lifted her stare from Sophie and beamed at the group as a whole.

"There's no rush. I'll always be here, waiting. I've nothing else to do." With those words, Elinor hurried back towards End

Cottage as quickly as she could make the others move, and found she was unable to bring herself to look back over her shoulder until she was quite sure they were out of sight of the alarming old woman.

Chapter Eight
Shadows And Lights

Elinor and Sophie arrived back at End Cottage later than intended, and with Sarah having been in a foul mood following Max's call Elinor fully expected a lecture about responsibility and acting like an adult. For once, luck was on her side. They returned home to find Sarah's car was strangely absent and waiting on the answerphone was a message for the girls. There had been some sort of crisis at the office, and as a result Sarah was going to be home late, so could Elinor be a dear and take care of things until she returned.

Having dodged a ticking off, Elinor was more than happy to oblige. She cooked supper, gave Sophie her bath and at eight 'o' clock exactly put her to bed. Sarah always told her daughter a story at bedtime, and Elinor was obliged to do the same, though this was one task she did not mind doing. She loved reading, and Sophie loved the way her cousin did different voices for each of the characters. After almost an hour Sophie, who seemed incapable of settling down, fell asleep, and Elinor, lulled into relaxation by the softly lit room, also drifted off into a dreamless state of oblivion.

Time ticked by. The sky turned from flaming red to star-light grey before surrendering to the all-enveloping black which swallowed up the world beyond the walls of End Cottage. Elinor remained asleep in the chair besides Sophie's bed as these changes swept by, but had she been awake, with no street lights to illuminate the road her home was situated on, she would still have missed the dark shape lurking at the edge of the property, looking at the barely lit building ahead.

With no sign of movement from within, the watcher swept towards the front door. It was locked, but this was no obstacle. Without pausing the visitor vanished from the front steps and re-appeared instantly on the far side of the door. Elinor twitched in her sleep as what few lights were on flickered erratically in the presence of the intruder drifting along the lower levels of the house.

Having finished searching the cellar and ground floor, the figure paused at the foot of the stairway that led up to where the unsuspecting Elinor and Sophie slept.

The door to Sophie's room was ajar through which a narrow beam of light from the landing shone in. Neither girl noticed this tiny ray of brightness being broken as the formless shadow glided past and continued on up to the attic. An unnatural quiet descended throughout the house, and whether it was this or a pressing feeling of foreboding which woke Elinor there was no telling, but from no-where, lunging into her otherwise imageless sleep, came the gaunt figure of a recently deceased Sophie, reaching out towards her, uttering in a voice of anguish,

"Help me, Elinor. You should have saved me."

With cold greying fingers stretching towards her, Elinor broke free of her slumber, and instantly looked down at her cousin to make sure it had been a nightmare. Thankfully, Sophie lay asleep, her soft breathing sounding like sweet music to the panicked babysitter.

Less enchanting was the noise which came next. It too was gentle, but in no way could be described as reassuring. From above, in her room, there came the unmistakable sound of something being heaved across the floor.

Her heart missed several beats as the adrenaline surge doubled her pulse rate in a split second. She was torn by indecision. Should she go up to investigate the noise or wait for help to come to her? She could phone for the police, but that would mean having to go down to the lower floor of the house which would leave Sophie alone and dangerously close to the unknown danger creeping about in the room above. She could stay where she was, but how did that help? The thing would still be snooping around upstairs and, worse still, when it decided to leave it would have to come past the very room she was hiding in. If she was spotted, there was no telling what reaction she might get, and Sophie again would be in the firing line. No, her only choice was to go and face it head on.

With each muscle in her entire body quivering, Elinor left the sleeping Sophie in the comparative safety of her room, taking the precaution to lock the door as she did so. That way, should she wake up, Sophie could not wander into trouble, but more importantly trouble could not get to her.

Slowly, she edged her way along the landing to the bottom of the stairs leading to her room and which looked unusually ominous as they reached up into the darkness above her.

Placing her foot onto the first step, Elinor forced herself to shut out her fears about what she walking into, and continued to climb up the mountain of shadow until she was there, outside the door to her own bedroom, which had taken on an aspect of terror unlike anything she had previously experienced.

Her mind was flooded with a stream of monstrous images, any one of which could be waiting on the far side of flimsy wooden partition separating them. The silence reverberated all around, and it occurred to Elinor that perhaps she had been mistaken. Maybe the noise was part of her dream, and in reality, she was stood, petrified, before nothing more than an empty room.

This thought had barely entered her head when she heard papers rustling. She had no choice but to continue on the path she had foolishly set out on.

With a shaky hand, Elinor grasped the door handle tightly, and with excessive force, threw the door open and burst into her room ready to confront the demon, but no-one was there, though there were signs someone had indeed been snooping.

The bedside lamp, which she had left on earlier, provided enough light for her to see the ransacked room by. The drawers in every unit were open, and their contents rifled. The notebooks she had stacked on her desk were scattered everywhere, and stray pieces of paper were strewn across every surface.

Elinor stepped into the room to survey the mess, unaware of the figure concealed in the space behind the door she had come through, and watched the unsuspecting teen from its hiding place.

Having forgotten her fears over coming face to face with an intruder, Elinor felt surprisingly irked. She had been ready to take on an undefined enemy and what had she been left with? A trashed room she was going to have to tidy up, preferably before her aunt returned home. She bent down to pick up the discarded items, and as she did so, from the corner of her eye, she saw it approaching.

A large black mist darted out from behind the door, engulfing Elinor and anything else it encountered as it headed for the door. As it swept past her, the warmth of Elinor's blood faded as invisible hands clutched at her, causing her breath to send clouds of condensation into the air as those bound within the passing shadow encircled her, desperately trying to latch onto something living. She heard the cries too, tormented, haunting cries for mercy, as along with the fleeing shadow they exited the house, leaving Elinor motionless on the floor.

Though she felt frozen to the core, she was up on her feet immediately following the shadow's departure, and took off after it. She thundered down both stairways, forgetting her cousin was fast asleep and locked in her room. On she went, with her quarry just out of reach. The erratic buzzing of the lights did not register as she saw the dark mist evaporate before the front door and then re-appear on the porch.

Ripping the door open, Elinor burst out of the house and made towards the road when two blinding circles of light swooped in front of her eyes, shattering the otherwise impenetrable night sky, dazzling her into a standstill. It took a while for her sight to recover, and by the time it had, both the lights and the prowler had disappeared. Elinor strained her eyes in vain as she tried to find any trace of the uninvited visitor, but she seemed to be the only being out in the village.

"Bugger," Elinor muttered under her breath.

With no light, Elinor did not see the person who approached from behind, and remained ignorant of their presence until a hand dropped down and grabbed hold of her shoulder. Elinor jumped half way out of her skin as she turned and saw in the glow of a small torch her aunt. She burst into a fit of relieved laughter as beheld the confused features of Sarah rather than the disfigured face of the creature she had been expecting to encounter.

"Elinor! What on earth are you doing out here in the middle of the night?"

"I could ask you the same question," Elinor answered rather more sharply. "We expected you back hours ago."

The pair headed back up towards the house.

"I would have been home sooner, but work dragged on for longer than I thought it would, then the car broke down in the next village, and unable to get a signal on my phone, I decided to leave the useless machine there and walk home. Perhaps now, you will answer my question. Why are you out in the street so late?" Quick as lightning, Elinor's brain came up with a reply.

"Rick told me about a takeaway nearby that does deliveries, so I ordered a pizza, but it's not turned up yet. I was checking to see if there was any sign of it, but no joy. The driver was probably using a satnav which can't locate Mournsby. I can't even find it on a map, so anyone using modern technology has no hope!"

Back in the house, Elinor bid a hasty good-night to her aunt and retreated to her room, which no longer felt particularly restful. On the way she unlocked Sophie's door and peeked in to check she had not been woken by Elinor's impersonation of an elephant charging about the property. Somehow, the little girl had slept through the entire drama, for which her babysitter was incredibly happy about. She might have been able to' explain why she was out of the house in the dead of night, but coming up with a reason for imprisoning Sophie in her room would be nigh on impossible.

The door to her room may have been open, but to Elinor it looked more sinister than it had before. She flicked on every light, checked behind each piece of furniture, investigated any shadowy corner and, much to her own hilarity, looked under the bed before finally consenting to close the door.

Though it was late, Elinor could not go to bed. She was still hyped up from the evenings unsettling events, and had the unenviable task of tidying up after her ghostly guest. Putting things back into order, she pondered over the stream of strange happenings Mournsby had sent her way. It was possible to come up with rational explanations for the majority of them, but tonight was not such a case.

Something had been inside the house. She labelled it a 'something' rather than a 'someone' for a couple of extremely simply reasons. Firstly, there was no sign of someone having broken in, and certainly from the way the trespasser exited the house, which she had witnessed with her own eyes, they had not broken out of it either. Then there was the speed at which the thing moved. It did not walk, run or use any apparent mortal means of moving about. It had drifted through the air, like a cloud caught on a strong wind. And the crying? She had not dreamt up those wailing voices which begged for help.

Of course, she had no answer for any of these questions, and neither did she know why her room had been searched. What had they been looking for and did they find it?

Without intending to, Elinor looked out of the window towards the graveyard, but the multitude of orbs were nowhere to be seen. In their place however, was something new. It appeared to be a lantern of some sort, as beams of gentle radiation shone out from it at several angles.

Elinor tracked its slow progress through the headstones as it swung gently in the hand of whatever was carrying it. Unlike her floating orbs, which darted about left, right and centre, the lantern was following a more defined route. The well-walked path she had spotted through the gates perhaps? She kept her stare on it until, obscured by the trees surrounding the deeper parts of the cemetery, it vanished. Elinor hastily drew the curtains.

She quickly got ready for bed, and, not entirely over the close encounter she had earlier, left the bedside light closest to her switched on as she huddled under her sheets, and went to sleep, missing the moment when the lantern bearer returned from the gloom and by the wall on the far side of the burial site, paused, before returning to its lair in the same way it had entered the cemetery to check that it's secret was still undiscovered.

Satisfied things were as they should be, the lantern and the one carrying it departed the scene, and the night was peaceful at last.

Chapter Nine
A Story Shared

Elinor woke early as usual after another night of disturbing dreams. The same images had danced in and out of her mind, but were now accompanied by the dark figure who roamed restlessly through the lands beyond the gates. For a moment she wondered why the lights were on, but the remembrance of the previous night rushed back into her mind, re-awakening the alarm she had felt. Before her mind could dwell on such things, Elinor got up, dressed and hurried downstairs. By now, she knew the location of each squeaky floorboard, and could edge her way past them with ease.

In the kitchen, a rather cutting note from her aunt was waiting on the table. She picked it up, and was hit by a wave of sickness as she read it.

"Elinor, I understand I have been asking a lot of you, but if you must have friends over, and you feel like a trip down memory lane, could you at least have the decency to tidy up afterwards? It was not exactly the highlight of my day coming home to find the place had apparently been hit by a whirlwind. I've made a start, but could you finish putting everything back where it belongs?"

The description of a whirlwind type mess greeting Sarah sent alarm bells ringing as it matched perfectly with how her room had been left following the intruder's search. She went from room to room and found every draw, cupboard and unit had been rummaged through. Papers, photos and documents were everywhere. As she put them away, Elinor noted most of what had been examined was in some way linked to their old lives. Anything relating to Mournsby had been discarded but anything older had been placed with great care in piles on the tops of tables and units. What had they been looking for? And did they find it? Elinor doubted it for her aunt, ever afraid of Max raiding the property in her absence, had entrusted documents such as birth certificates, rental agreements and financial papers to the care of her brother.

By the time she had the house back in order Sarah was up and, fortunately, in a better frame of mind than she had been when she wrote the note to her niece. In fact, she appeared to have forgotten about the mess and her reprimand, so finding the house neat and tidy at such an early hour improved her mood further. In an attempt to avoid a further punishment, Elinor kept quiet as to the reasons for her having cleaned the house without being asked to and was duly rewarded.

It was Saturday, and as a thank you for staying late the night before, Frank had given his sister the day off work. She was going to nip to the village she had been forced to leave her car in then take Sophie into town for the day. Elinor was welcome to go too, but Sarah thought she might prefer to spend the time on her own, or in her own way.

Instantly, Elinor knew she had been handed a golden opportunity. She wanted to find out more about what was going on around Mournsby, and this was her best chance of doing so. The research she was intending to do was dark, morbid stuff and not suitable material for young Sophie, and this was the first day Elinor had been free from watching her cousin.

Her biggest problem was where to start? Mournsby might have been small, but there was no internet access, no records office, nothing where she could begin her search. It seemed asking the locals was her one hope, but that too was not as simple as it should have been.

There was no missing the strange, contagious memory loss which had spread throughout the residents of the village. They struggled to remember events from the previous day, so what were the chances of anyone being able to recall incidents from decades ago?

With the rate she was progressing at, Elinor knew she had to pick somewhere to begin otherwise she'd never get started, so, she selected two people who she knew reasonably well to speak with first.

Once Sarah and Sophie had left for town, Elinor headed straight to Rick and Emma's grandparent's house. She was on good terms with both, and quizzing them about their pasts was less likely to arouse suspicion than her interrogating the other neighbours.

The welcome was not as warm as it usually was. Emma opened the door, and immediately Elinor could tell something was wrong. Her friend was pale and quiet, and she opened the door as if expecting an axe wielding loony to be on the step. Her nerves eased as she saw Elinor.

"Oh, it's you."

"I'm happy to see you too!" Elinor said with sarcasm. "Are you okay, Em?" It was clear to see the girl was not okay. She still kept the door half closed, and her cheerful air was nowhere to be seen.

Before Emma could answer, Rick joined his sister.

"Hey, Elle. Has she told you we're grounded? Not allowed out for the whole day." Elinor could not help but smile at the idea of the sixteen and eighteen year olds being under house arrest, and in Mournsby of all places. Whatever the brother and sister had done it would have been a far worse punishment to have ordered them to spend the day out in the village where they would be cut off from all forms of entertainment. "Are you coming in?" Rick asked.

"Gran said we couldn't go out to meet our friends," Emma said.

"Right, and we've not gone out. Elinor has come to us, and it would be bad manners to turn away a visitor without offering them a drink."

The friends made their way into the kitchen, and Emma set about getting them some drinks.

"So what did you do to get yourselves grounded?"

"Nothing," Emma spat out hurriedly, making her sound far more guilty than she was.

"Really?"

"Really."

"Relax, will you sis. Elinor's not here to arrest us. The truth is we didn't do anything, but gran and gramps think we did."

"So, what do they think you did?" Elinor asked taking her drink.

"It's mad. Weird even," Rick continued. "Which is why I can't understand Emma's nervousness. Stuff like this should be right up her street. Shortly after we got back yesterday evening, the oldies decided to go to the local pub for a drink after the barbecue. Emma and I took advantage of the left over burgers and food and had ourselves a bit of a picnic.

"When they got home, gran came bursting into the garden and went off on one about our being drunk and trashing the house. We did not know what she was going on about, but we went in to see the scene of crime and the place looked as if a tornado had blown through the house. There were papers everywhere. Anyway, they refused to hear our side of things, ordered us to tidy it up and banned us from going out for the whole of today."

Rick saw instantly the alteration in Elinor's expression as he described the state their house had been left in, and from her lack of surprise, Emma quickly sensed their companion knew more about it than they did.

"What?"

"You know what happened."

"I don't."

"Was it you who made the mess?"

"Don't be bloody stupid"

"All right, it wasn't you, but you damn well know who it was."

"I don't."

"But you know something."

Elinor did not reply. Confirming their beliefs would lead to a thousand other confusing questions she would then have to answer, but she could not leave them without an explanation. She let out a sigh of exasperation. The time had come to share the story of what had been going on around her since her arrival in Mournsby.

"All right. I do know something, but it's kind of complicated. Look, I'll tell you everything I know, or suspect, or think is going on, but keep quiet until I've finished. It's a mad enough story without interruptions making it harder to share."

So, Elinor revealed all. She told Emma and Rick about the lights in the cemetery, the haunting dreams and ethereal voices. She then explained how, like their house, her home had been raided during the evening, but unlike them, she had caught sight of the one responsible.

Once finished, a silence of stunned disbelief filled the room. Elinor gulped down the last of her drink, fearful her two friends would find her tale so fantastic, they would find it impossible to believe a word of what she had said, but her concerns were eased as expressions of curiosity and anxious excitement spread over their previously stunned faces.

Rick initially reasoned away many of the things Elinor described, but when added together reason seemed to have little to do with any of it, and he certainly could not explain what had occurred in both houses the night before. Emma on the other hand accepted Elinor's story without question.

"I've thought since the start there was something odd going on here. Look at the way no-one seems able to remember their own name. Gran and gramps have to be reminded who we are on a daily basis, and then there was last night." Rick agreed it was odd, but he was still far from ready to believe supernatural forces were running amok in Mournsby. He wanted proof, to see it with his own eyes, and Elinor was happy to assist.

"Well, if that's what you want, that's what you'll get. Come over to my place tonight, the pair of you, and we'll keep watch for those who go walking in the graveyard after dark."

Elinor headed home with a smile on her face. This was partly due to the anticipation she felt about the vigil she was going to hold with her friends, but mainly because of how quickly Rick's air of bravado faded when she suggested they search Mournsby for spectres in the dead of night. She arrived back at End Cottage where, to her surprise, she saw a car parked in the spot where her aunt's vehicle was usually left. She walked up the path, found the front door was unlocked, and walked in.

Half expecting to come face to face with the same uninvited guest she'd encountered the day before, Elinor held her breath. She almost collapsed with relief when her aunt called out from the kitchen.

"Is that you, Elinor?"

"Who else." she answered, pausing in the doorway of the room, where she found her aunt surrounded by mountains of paperwork.

"How was town?" Sarah sighed loudly as she moved one collection of papers to the side and dragged another forward.

"We didn't get that far. We were towed to the garage, and in the middle of sorting out a courtesy car, Frank phoned me to say yesterday's deal needed reworking and asked me to go over some points in the contract ready for Monday morning. So, Sophie and I had to come home. I thought it might have been her just now. I told her to be home by four."

Sarah's words caused panic to fill Elinor's heart. She wondered if Sophie had decided to try and find her, and was out in the village somewhere, lost.

"Where is Sophie?" Considering she had mentioned her barely ten seconds before, Sarah looked at Elinor as if she had no idea what she was talking about.

"Sophie?"

"Yes, Sophie. You know; your daughter. Seven years old, about so high, blonde hair."

"I know who she is. She was bored hanging around the house with no-one to play with, when one of the neighbours called by and invited her out. A nice lady. Apparently she met Sophie in the village one day, and decided to come by and introduce herself. She told me if there was ever anything she could do to help me out, I was just to say the word. She loves children."

Elinor's fears had been far from eased as her aunt spoke of the elderly helper, and at the last three words of her statement, she was struggling to keep them hidden.

"Did she have a name, this beacon of assistance for single parents?" The sarcasm in her voice was overlooked as Sarah was so preoccupied with her work, but she did acknowledge the question.

"Yes. Now, what was it? It was a funny name. Ah, Mrs Barrowhyde."

Elinor turned for the door with such speed it attracted the attention of her otherwise inattentive aunt.

"Where are you off to in such a rush?" Elinor thought fast. She could hardly say Sophie was in the clutches of a terrifying entity, because apart from Mrs Barrowhyde being to the casual observer, nothing more than a slightly batty old woman, Elinor had no idea why she was left cold by the thought of Sophie being in her care.

"I'm going to fetch Sophie. You wanted her home by four, and it's almost that now. Tea will be late, which means Sophie will go to bed past her bedtime, won't settle, and will be a grumpy so-and-so tomorrow due to lack of sleep. Is that what you want?" Without delay, Sarah ordered Elinor to continue with her task, and she would put the supper on.

Never before had Elinor walked with such determination as she did on that march to Mrs Barrowhyde's house. It was foolish, even to her, but the feeling that time was of the essence would not go away. She could not begin to imagine what had come over her aunt. Before the move to Mournsby she would never had allowed Sophie to go off with a stranger, even an apparently harmless one in the guise of an old woman.

In record time she reached the long, winding driveway of the Barrowhyde residence. The entrance, cut into the stone wall which ran unbroken in every other direction, was far from welcoming.

Standing there, Elinor felt she was about to cross some sort of forbidden boundary, and the consequences of doing so would be severe. Yet, she had no choice. She had done everything she could think of to avoid this place, but she was bought back to them time after time. Her concerns for her own safety were overridden by those she had for Sophie, and knowing she would regret doing so, Elinor accepted the curse, and entered the property.

The grounds were extensive, this much was obvious from the start as the drive wound down the avenue of trees which lined its sides, and vanished from view amongst them. Close to the entrance was an old, wooden sign with the name of the house carved into the half rotten timber.

"Larchend," Elinor said to herself, instantly wishing she had not spoken, because though she barely whispered the name, her voice sounded abnormally loud amid the ear piercing silence she was in the centre of.

Keen as she was to locate her cousin and escape back to the safety of End Cottage, there was something about the atmosphere of Larchend, which prevented Elinor from moving too quickly. It was like being in enemy territory, and too sudden a movement would betray her presence to those intent on hunting her. Taking such care though did allow her to survey the gardens she was creeping through.

Something was not right with them, but she was so busy jumping at her own footsteps she was not been able to put her finger on what was out of place initially. Then it came to her. It was the trees. They were almost dead. Every other tree in the village, and probably the county, was in full bloom, covered in a mass of green leaves and full of nesting birds. The trees she passed under were colourless, thin and the few leaves they had were dry and rattled a warning of doom as the wind blew through them. This led Elinor to note the lack of birds present, and, despite being so close to fields, not a single note of their songs could be heard. The more she looked, the more she observed. The grass was not green and bright, but a sickly shade of brown. Despite there being no leaves to block its path, the sun seemed somehow dimmed as it shone down from above. Even the sky had a sort of sepia coloured tint to it.

These observations were added to as, lost amongst the untamed lawns, Elinor saw signs of habitation, though these too appeared to have been from a time long since passed. There was a child's swing, or to be accurate, the remnants of what had been a child's swing. The metal frame was dull and rusting, and the seat of the swing hung limply from the one half of the chain which was still connected.

Other toys began to reveal themselves to the sharp eyed teenager. There were bicycles, trikes and a slide, all in a similar state of decay as the swing was. Leaving them behind, Elinor was filled with a sense of sadness and loss, a reaction she could not explain. She had no chance to think on these feelings further for quite unexpectedly she found herself standing before Larchend House, and its aura made her previous worries seem trivial.

The house was old, early Victorian, maybe older. It was three stories high, or so it seemed, but Elinor quickly spotted the tiny windows in what she assumed was the attic space of the roof. The house was typical of its type, but like the grounds surrounding it, the building had a faded look to it. The brick work was grimy, and the windows which decorated its walls were layered in years of dirt. What fragments of paintwork remained were peeling off the disintegrating wood beneath them.

Moved closer, Elinor tried to peek in through the windows, but between the muck smeared over the glass and the frayed curtains hanging inside, it was a pointless effort. At the bottom of the steps leading up to the front door were more abandoned toys; another bike, a few footballs and a torn kite lay forlornly on the porch. The idea of Sophie being on the far side of the door caused Elinor concern. Everything was so rickety, rotten and plain dangerous in its appearance, she wondered how anyone could hope to set foot in the place without some section of the house dropping on top of them. Combined with the fact it was owned by Mrs Barrowhyde, easily the most frightening person for miles around, meant Elinor could react in one way.

"Sophie!"

The call went unanswered. Elinor tried again.

"Sophie." Still only silence replied. "Is there anyone there? Sophie! Where the hell are you?"

Inwardly, she scolded herself for using the word 'hell' in such a location.

"Great," she muttered under her breath. "Here I am, stood in the middle of the set for every ghost story ever written, and what do I do? Alert anyone and anything close by to my presence. Idiot! Sophie." Elinor turned around in a circle, scanning the area for any trace of the missing child, but could find none.

Her nerves began to get the better of her, as did the silence of the property and its aged hue. She faced the house once more and was greeted by the staring, emotionless eyes of Mrs Barrowhyde, watching her from one of the lower windows. The ghost-like apparition sent Elinor flailing backwards with a gasp of pure shock, but worse still was that within the blink of an eye the woman was gone. Elinor cast her eyes from pane to glass pane, but found no trace of her, when from directly behind a voice said,

"Can I do something for you?"

Elinor, whose nerves were already shattered, struggled to supress the scream which burst erupted in her lungs. Mrs Barrowhyde seemingly did not care about the effect her arrival had on the teenager, and simply repeated her question.

"Can I do something for you?" Elinor's voice squcaked a reply.

"Sorry for the interruption, but I've come to collect Sophie."

Mrs Barrowhyde's air of indifference changed to the one she had first viewed the girl with when they met. One of suspicion.

"I've been sent to fetch her home. It's time for her tea."

"Oh, so now she wants her back, does she?" Mrs Barrowhyde said in a tone which sounded more like an accusation than a comment, and one, which considering she had gone to Sarah with the offer of help, threw Elinor.

"Is she here?" she stuttered.

After what seemed like an eternity, during which Mrs Barrowhyde studied her with great intent, the woman replied.

"Yes. She's here." The admission was of great relief to Elinor, but as she did not produce her cousin, it did nothing to move things along.

The conversation remained at a standstill for some time until, wondering if Mrs Barrowhyde had fallen into some kind of trance Elinor tried a different, more direct approach.

"Sophie!" It too failed. With her cousin being noticeable by her absence and Mrs Barrowhyde in her hypnotic state, Elinor was running out of ideas. "Sophie." Without warning, the house owner snapped back to reality and in a voice which was no more than a whisper said,

"Sophie. Time to go home." At once the youngster appeared at the front door and hurried over to her caller.

"Must I go? I've had such a good time." Elinor took hold of Sophie's hand.

"Good for you, but home." She had not meant to be so abrupt, but she was desperate to leave the penetrating gaze of Mrs Barrowhyde. Her request did not go down well.

Though she was normally well behaved, Sophie could, if the mood took her, throw the most monumental tantrums, and seeing the unmistakable flicker of anger flare up in the seven year olds eyes as her muscles tensed up, Elinor knew she and her neighbour were about to be treated to one such outburst. But the hissy fit never came. As her face turned scarlet in rage, Mrs Barrowhyde stopped the firework display before it got started. She stroked the child's hair.

"You should go home, Sophie, but you are always welcome here. We will have plenty of other chances to continue our games, and next time, as you've been so good, I'll let you play with the house." Sophie's colour returned to normal and her face lit up with delight.

"Oh, thank you. I'll be back soon."

"Well, you'll have to see what your mum says about that," Elinor cut in swiftly before any definite plans were arranged between the pair of them. Sophie gave a dismissive huff, which was quite unlike her.

"Mummy won't mind. She's far too busy with work." Mrs Barrowhyde, to Elinor's surprise, seemed to agree with her.

"Maybe Elinor wants to spend time with you."

"She doesn't want me hanging around. She's got her friends, I've have no-one."

The words wounded Elinor more deeply than she thought possible, but her pain did not hinder her observational skills. There was no missing the gleeful smirk on the woman's face at Sophie's words, renewing her desire to leave Larchend as quickly as possible. Taking hold of Sophie's hand, Elinor began to drag her back towards the road and in turn, safety.

"Thank you again for your help, Mrs Barrowhyde. We'll be going now." Sophie continued to wave and call out her farewells until Larchend and its resident were out of sight. All the way home, she babbled on about how much fun her day had been, and continued to do so once they reached End Cottage.

Over supper, Elinor and Sarah endured a constant stream of stories about everything she had done during her time at Larchend, but only Elinor was really listening with any degree of interest. There was nothing remarkable in Sophie's activities themselves, but her description of the house and grounds did not tally with Elinor's recollection of the place.

"The house is beautiful, all painted up. Her garden is huge, and full of toys. There were swings and a slide, it was like a park, with lots of trees and hiding places to play in, but my favourite was the doll's house."

Sarah, ignoring Elinor's usual expression of revulsion that appeared whenever the topic of toy houses came up, turned to Sophie.

"A doll's house? Wow."

"Yeah. It was Mrs Barrowhyde's when she was little. It's really old, like her. She wouldn't let me play with it today though. She said I had to prove myself trustworthy first, but she did show it to me, and before I left she gave this."

Sophie pulled a small figure out of her pocket and showed it to the others. It was a doll, the perfect size for going in a child's doll house, but upon closer inspection, there was something unnervingly familiar about its features. There was no mistaking it; the doll was a miniature version of Sophie. Its clothes, hair and features were those of her cousin, only on a smaller scale.

"Mrs Barrowhyde said I must have my own special doll. Everyone who gets to play with the house has to have their own doll."

Why did that statement sound so sinister?

The attachment Sophie developed for the toy was equally worrying. She carried it with her until bedtime, and then she sat it on the small table at the side of her bed, but these wonderings soon disappeared from Elinor's mind as the time for Rick and Emma's arrival neared.

Her aunt had no objections to the friends coming over, but extracted a promise from her niece they would keep the noise down. Apart from Sophie being in bed, after a few days of unending work, Sarah wanted an early night, and did not fancy being woken up by three rowdy teenagers. Vowing to keep the noise to a minimum, Sarah went off to her room, leaving Elinor curtain twitching in anticipation of Rick and Emma's arrival.

The sun had set, and the sky decidedly darkened by the time the brother and sister knocked at the door. Elinor's nerves sparked wildly, half from fear about what the three of them were about to do, and half out of excitement about delving into the unknown, and she found it hard to keep her promise about being quiet. Rick and Emma were in a similar state of mind, and having been hushed by Elinor they made it to the seclusion of the attic.

With the door shut, the need for absolute silence ended. Elinor's room was in such a position that short of tap dancing across the floor, neither sleeper on the floor below would be disturbed by their movements. The repressed excitement could be contained no more.

"A late night vigil!" Emma chuckled enthusiastically. "It's something I've always wanted to take part in."

"You mean your dream has been to sit up in the dark with the sole aim of keeping watch for dead people?!" Rick teased.

"Pack it in. Elinor's as up for this as I am." It was obvious Emma's deduction was right. Rick exhaled heavily with feigned resignation.

"Why don't I know anyone normal?" Despite his words, Rick was as curious about what the night might bring them as his counterparts were, though he suspected all they'd get for their efforts would be sleep deprivation, stiff necks and kinks in their backs having sat perched by a small window for hours on end.

With a selection of drinks and snacks to hand, Elinor went over her experiences in more detail, and hinted what Rick and Emma should look out for.

At the time of their occurring, Elinor's encounters had seemed perfectly sane, but as she expressed them out loud, she could not help thinking she sounded half crazy, and if that was how she viewed herself, what would the others think?

Thankfully, Emma believed every word of the account given, and Rick, deciding as the lunatics had him out numbered, offered up no opinion and simply went along with them. But even their shared interest in the mysterious lights haunting the graveyard was not enough to stop the irresistible force that was sleep. By Midnight Emma was out cold and Rick followed soon after. Elinor too, who was the most motivated of the group finally succumbed, but the nightmare she plunged straight into did nothing to dispel her worries over what was happening around her.

It started out in the usual way. She was on the streets of Mournsby as night descended. The elements engulfed the area around where she stood, but this was where the first alteration to her dream took place. Usually she was stood before the cemetery gates and felt as if she had been guided there, but this time she was not being led to her destination, but rather chased. The wind was blowing a gale, but made no sound. The trees bowed before its wrath but not a single leaf rustled in protest, and as she looked towards the protective shelter of End Cottage she found the path home consumed by darkness. Something was coming for her.

Every instinct screamed at her to run, though her head and heart told her to stand firm it was her first inclination which triumphed. Elinor bolted from the spot, not sure what she was running from never mind where she was heading to. It was gaining on her, the same feeling of immediate danger she experienced the night she had come into contact with the intruder at her home. Its fingers locked down onto her shoulder, jerking her with such force it caused her to stumble and she tumbled to the ground.

Elinor knew instantly where she was. Rising above the free growing grass she could see the metal work of the gates leading to Mournsby's graveyard. Elinor's heart pounded as the deadly intentions of her pursuer loomed closer.

In an attempt to escape the murderous blow, Elinor scrambled across the verge, and in desperation grabbed hold of the shaking gates. The padlock split in two and the chain landed beside the cowering girl as the bar she held was wrenched free from her hand and the gates swung wide open. The malevolent being suddenly withdrew as, with the barrier gone, those who dwelled in the graveyard were able to leave their prison.

From out of the shadows the lights appeared, rushing towards the stricken girl, calling her name in voices so unearthly there was no denying they were of ghostly origin.

Swiftly as the cloud behind her disappeared, another replaced it, though this one waited before her, glowing softly as the inhabitants of the cemetery gathered around. Elinor did her best to keep from raising her eyes up to the scene before her, but they were seemingly beyond her control and as she looked towards her unwelcome but still remaining companions she saw not an inexplicable ball of light but a white swathe of material draped over a colourless arm reaching towards her, and all the time they continued to call to her.

"Elinor." Her name reverberated on the night air, which seemed to be closing in around her. "Elinor," they whispered as the lifeless fingers stretched out to touch her. "Elinor!"

At the third call, Elinor jumped, her sudden movement forcing her not only to wake up but also to slip from the chair she had fallen asleep in. Her crashing to the floor in turn woke the unconscious Emma and Rick, who were less than impressed at being disturbed at so ridiculous an hour. They grumbled about it being too early to get up, and quickly fell back to sleep, leaving Elinor alone wide awake. Before she joined them, she got up and left the room. Rick and Emma might long to have a few more hours lost in the imaginary worlds of their dreams, but Elinor had no desire to return to a land only she and the dead had access to.

Yet, in spite of her nightmares, or maybe because of them, her desire to go to the place responsible for her nightly terrors was stronger than ever. Why? There had to be a reason. She hoped there was, otherwise her dreams and supposedly paranormal visions had to be a sign of madness. Was she mad? It was possible. She alone had witnessed the spectral light show. She was the one who dreamt about being followed by apparitions. She saw things differently from everyone else. Mrs Barrowhyde's house was a prime example. Sophie described it as beautifully decorated, but to Elinor's eyes it had been a dilapidated wreck. Yet, she was not the only one to feel that something dreadful hung over Mournsby. Everyone she met sensed it, mentioned it or was affected by it.

A light suddenly came on in Elinor's mind as another revelation dawned on her. She may have been the one affected most by the village's spooky goings-on, but she was the least affected by Mournsby itself. Somehow, she had penetrated its mask of rural tranquillity and uncovered, in part, whatever it was that held it and the residents under its sway. How? Why? And to what end? She had to find out and resolved to do just that, no matter what it took. The question was where to start? The answer to that had already been provided.

There was one location that had gone out of its way to attract the girl's attention since the very day she had arrived. The one place she was led back to time and time again. Elinor realized where her hunt for the truth had to begin, and it seemed to have been decided long before she came to know Mournsby existed.

"The cemetery."

Chapter Ten

Looking To The Past

Leaving her compatriots safely asleep, and taking great care not to alert Sophie or her aunt, Elinor exited End Cottage. How she secretly hoped for a groaning door hinge or whining floorboard to give the game away and for one of the sleepers to discover her antics. That would give her an excuse to call of the foolhardy adventure she was about to undertake. For once the building kept quiet, and those within it appeared to be dead to the world.

"Stupid description," Elinor hissed reminding herself where she was making for. Indeed, it did seem like Fate intended her to complete the trip she had set out on as not so much as passing farmer was on the street to enquire what she was doing out at such an early hour.

The morning was a cool one and embraced Elinor with its chilly arms as she neared her destination. Her apprehension grew with each step. Had everyone in the world been whisked away during the night in order there should be nothing to hinder her trip? She tried to slow her progress down by deliberately taking small steps, but Elinor arrived at the gateway in no time at all.

She stopped a few metres short of the ancient entranceway and took a shaky breath. It did not help. A mix of emotions swirled within her, guilt being the dominating one. She was, at the end of the day, on the verge of violating sacred ground.

"Oh, get on with it." Before her capacity for reasoning returned and made her go home, Elinor forced her legs to carry her forward until she was back there where it all began; nose pressed up against the gates of Mournsby's cemetery.

They were locked, as usual, by the rusty chain and padlock, but if some supernatural power wanted her to come to this unlikely spot, why could she not pass beyond a man-made piece of metal?

Wondering whether there was some clue concealed beneath the layers of oxidization, Elinor took hold of the lock, intending to rub the rust away, but as her fingers touched it the padlock clicked open in her hand with such ease it was as if the lock had been made that very day.

Elinor pulled the chain away from the railings, allowing it to drop almost silently into the thick grass on which she stood, and pushed the gates open. They were not as willing to surrender as their shackles had been, but they eventually opened with remarkable ease, considering their age.

Intimidating as the graveyard had been before, once opened, Elinor found it more frightening than ever. Maybe it was because just as the gates prevented her and others from accessing the cemetery, they had also ensured whatever roamed amongst the gravestones was kept in.

"How thick are you?" Elinor said firmly. "If there are spirits in there, they are hardly going to be impeded by a mere gate!"

Having run out of excuses for not proceeding, Elinor held her breath, shut her eyes and hurriedly swapped the mortal realm for that of the dead.

"I am not afraid. I am not afraid," she lied to herself, carving a way through the massively overgrown greenery, thinking of Rick, Emma, Sarah and Sophie back at the house, warm and snug and safe as they slept, unaware of what the impetuous teenager was up to. She wondered in what fit of insanity creeping about in an abandoned burial plot, at dawn, and alone, had seemed a good idea. Anything might happen to her, and for she was not referring to anything otherworldly.

The graveyard was so old there was a good chance some of the graves had subsided. There was little possibility of her spotting any such crevice in the ground with the grass being so long. She could easily break an ankle. She might fall and knock herself out on one of the headstones or worse still, supposing one of the graves had completely collapsed in on itself? Imagine, plummeting into an unseen chasm, to lay there for eternity, never to be found. No-one knew where she had gone, and who would select the old cemetery as a starting point for a search?

She pictured herself trapped there, deep in the dark earth, stuck in a hole already occupied by some other unfortunate soul's remains. She'd starve to death slowly until all that remained would be the skeleton she landed beside and her own bony frame. The mere thought made her ill, but she pressed on despite these misgivings because finally, she was on the track way which had been trampled flat by whoever walked there at night.

With a more secure footing beneath her, Elinor relaxed slightly as it dawned on her she had been holding her breath since entering the grounds.

The air was disquietingly calm, but at the same time, Elinor was sure it carried unheard screams, cries born out of torment and eternal anguish which tainted the otherwise serene atmosphere.

The path wound deeper into the older parts of the cemetery. Along the way, Elinor read the inscriptions on the headstones. Many had been worn away in the years since their carving, but some were still legible. There was nothing particularly outstanding in any of them, or so she thought to begin with but as she went on, Elinor noticed something was missing. The earliest date she could make out 1859, the other stones followed on from there. There was nothing remarkable about that; the cemetery must have come into use around that time. Until 1875 those who died were of various ages ranging from babies who were days old to those who reached their eighties.

Then, abruptly the children stopped appearing. Every stone from 1875 onwards marked where an adult was buried. Some were double plots where husband and wife lay together forever, but every last grave was that of a grown up. There were no children at all. Elinor had no wish to imagine the premature death of any youngster, but historically there was a high rate of death in children due to disease and poor diet, and based on the age of the cemetery itself, finding such graves should have been the norm. But there was not one. Where had the children gone?

It was conceivable that as Mournsby was so remote, and jobs in the area were few and far between, many had moved to more prosperous towns, but that was not enough to account for the complete absence of children's graves.

Without warning, the track ended and Elinor found herself stood before a large mausoleum. It was undeniably the resting place of some wealthy family for it was expensively built and ornately decorated. Large stone pillars supported the towering roof, and on either side of the door leading into the vault were a pair of beautifully sculpted, if oddly un-weathered, angels standing guard inside the iron railings surrounding the spot. It was here the path of crushed grass led. No other grave had the tell-tale signs of being frequently visited. The big question was why that particular place and no other? The next question to be answered was who was doing the visiting?

Her wonderings were brought to an abrupt halt as from behind she heard the sound of movement. There was no missing it. From her rear and to the left she heard something pushing through the thick grass. She looked nervously towards it but could see nothing. The noise reached her ears again, only closer than it was before. She turned with caution in the direction from which her predator approached. Still she could see no-one or nothing. But there it was. Yes, as the noise repeated itself she saw a section of grass twitch in agitation. Grabbing a medium sized branch which had fallen at some point in time from one of the trees, Elinor stepped towards the spy. The line between predator and prey blurred as she lifted her make shift club into the air.

"Come out," she ordered. "I'm armed." Another wave of disturbance swam through the greenery. "Have it your own way." She smashed the branch down roughly in the area she assumed her snooping guest was in, and succeeded in forcing her enemy out into the open. A pheasant soared up into the sky with a shriek, causing Elinor to jump half out of her skin.

The morbid seriousness of her situation was temporarily relieved as she gave into a fit of nervous laughter, but turning back to the mausoleum, Elinor came face to face with another girl. The undetected arrival of another trespasser jolted Elinor, with heart stopping speed.

"It's beautiful, don't you think?" the stranger said.

Elinor, who struggled to recover her voice, examined the girl in astonishment. She was a little younger than herself, with long dark hair which was swept back under a thick red ribbon. Her complexion appeared unusually pale, all the more so thanks to her raven coloured hair. With every part of her being quivering, Elinor's reply was somewhat jittery.

"Yes, I suppose it is." The girl, seeing how shaky Elinor was, continued.

"Sorry, did I scare you?" Elinor nodded. "I didn't mean to do so. It's a gift I have, though as you're the person caught off guard, you probably wouldn't agree with me." Elinor laughed.

"Well, I have to congratulate you. You've got it down to a fine art. I didn't hear a thing. It must have taken a lot of practice to be able to move about like that."

"Oh no," the new comer said. "It comes quite naturally."

The more she spoke to her, the more Elinor thought there was something odd about her new acquaintance, something entirely obvious but what it was escaped her recognition.

"It's a shame really," the pale figure continued, looking at the mausoleum.

"What is?"

"That people build such great monuments to the dead when there are so many among the living in need of help."

"I guess it's a way of remembering their loved ones."

"That's well and good, but often things which should be left in the past endure and those which should be remembered become lost. There is little point in honouring the departed if what they taught us in their lives, or their deaths, is ignored and allowed to fade. Without the lessons of the past, the future is doomed."

The conversation was as depressing as the graveyard, and Elinor was unable to respond to the girl's remark.

"How have you found Mournsby?" Elinor could easily answer that question.

"The name says it all. The village is practically dead." This, however, did not lead to the response she expected.

"It's not the village that's dead, but it does mourn what is, and lives in fear of that which not even Death can touch." Elinor tensed up at the words, for it appeared as if this apparently ordinary girl, who looked no different than herself, knew about the terrible secret haunting Mournsby. Elinor noticed the girl was monitoring her reactions with great care.

"I see you know what it is I am speaking of."

"Yes," Elinor stammered. "Erm, no. Well, not exactly."

The secret keeper stepped forward until she was face to face with the teenager.

"But you could find out, and quite easily too. Many have been waiting for your return, and are depending upon your courage, for you alone have the power to set them free and to keep further innocents from falling victim to the Mournsby Curse."

Elinor became alarmed at the word 'courage'. Courage, in whatever context it was used, implied some kind of danger, and danger was never a good thing. Worse still, it had been used in combination with the equally unappealing word 'curse'. It was a far from comforting thought.

"Sorry. What curse? Granted, Mournsby is a tad weird in its atmosphere, but that's probably because nobody's left its limits since the turn of the century. And I don't mean the one just gone either."

"Mournsby is the way it is because of its history. A history that refuses to stay in the past and until the link between it and the present is severed the future is bound to the same fate. There is but one person who can break the cycle. As we speak, another life hangs in the balance. History will repeat itself until the one with the power to bring the dead home acknowledges who they are and steps forward."

With open mouth, Elinor stood lost for words although her mind was full of questions, all of which over ran her sense of rationality. The distant sound of a car starting broke the stand-off.

"I must go," the young stranger said with a hint of fear in her voice.

"You can't leave. I've got so much to ask you. Why are you telling this to me? I don't understand. What am I supposed to do?"

"Everything you need in order to complete your task is already in your possession, you just have to see it, but remember; it is by looking to the past you will find a way to secure the future." She shot a hurried glance at the mausoleum they were stood before.

"The past can tell us much, and once we know where to start the rest follows quite easily."

Elinor's spirits rose as she saw why the girl was so obsessed with the burial site beside them. It was a clue as to where she should begin her search, but she still felt overwhelmed.

"There is little more I can say to guide you, but this may help in some way. Do not be fooled into thinking the number of lost souls is accurate. In such cases, there is always a victim, a sacrifice, who goes unrecorded. Find this person and you will discover the name of the one you seek. But, be warned, time is short and before long Mournsby will again live up to its name." Elinor leant back against a headstone, numb.

"I can't do it. I can't do this alone."

"You are not alone, and never have been. There are many who will stand beside you, who already do so. You are loved, and so, protected."

"I know. I owe Sarah a lot. She took me on despite her husband's objections."

"I did not mean your aunt. You've been helped by many you have never seen."

The teenager's eyes sparked with curiosity.

"Who are you talking about?"

"Time will reveal all. You just have to know where to begin." Elinor repeated the clue she had been given.

"Look to the past."

Elinor was about to thank the stranger, but she had vanished in the exact same manner she arrived in; without warning or sound. Elinor scanned the area but found no trace of her.

Puzzled, she decided to focus on one conundrum at a time and went back to examining the mausoleum. What information could she possibly glean from the final resting place of the one-time local big-wigs? The car engine accelerating away told Elinor she was no longer the only resident on the move in the village, and she had to make the best use of what time was left available to her.

Surprisingly, the small gate into the family's gravesite was not locked. Elinor walked up to the doorway of the chamber where the coffins were laid and read the names inscribed on the large stone slabs on either side of them where she discovered her first real clue.

The family name was, to her shock and dismay, one that was regrettably familiar to her. The mausoleum belonged to the Barrowhydes. Over the centuries, many of Mrs Barrowhyde's ancestors had lived and died in and around Mournsby, and had then been placed in the tomb Elinor was trespassing in, but the last of them had been sealed in the vaults in 1879. The cemetery had been in use long after that date. So where had the Barrowhyde's gone to?

The answer was in the final three names of those laid to rest there. Each was sad in its own right, but collectively they spoke of a sudden and brutal ending of a great family.

The first of the three named was a young girl, just five years old, when she met her end and it seemed her death had been far from natural. Under her name, Mary Barrowhyde, and the dates which marked out her short existence were the words 'Beloved daughter and sister. Tragically taken'. She died in 1875. Next to follow in 1879 was a Mr Timothy Barrowhyde, the father of Mary, Elinor assumed. He too was unusually young at the time he met his maker, and but three months later his wife followed. Had the grief of losing their daughter left them so broken hearted they died as a result? Was the reason the Barrowhyde's mausoleum had ceased being used been that the family line had come to an end, and so there was no-one left to bury there?

It was possible, but no. No, that was not right. Mary's memorial plaque mentioned a sister. Where had she gone? Was the present Mrs Barrowhyde a distant relative who moved back to the village of her people, for whatever reason? Did the one woman Elinor feared hold the solution to the riddles she was besieged by? With sounds of activity drifting towards her from the village, Elinor knew she had to go as with every second that passed her likelihood of being caught increased, but at last she had somewhere to begin her search.

Keeping to the same route she had followed to the Barrowhyde plot, Elinor made her way back to the main gates, pulled them shut with the same ease with which they had opened, wrapped the chain around them and clicked the padlock shut. All was as it had been when she first arrived there that morning. The few hints she had picked up filled her with a new energy, but with it came a sense of rapidly nearing danger which could not be avoided, and she, Elinor, was going to have face head on.

She raced back to End Cottage, tore up to her room and pounced on the unconscious Emma and Rick.

"Wake up, sleepy heads!" Elinor sang loudly, shaking them roughly until they could not hope to ignore her. "We've got work to do." Once she was sure she had their undivided attention, Elinor shared her story about the adventure in the graveyard, but it was clear to her, based on their expressions of bewilderment, the brother and sister were not sure if they were awake or stuck in a dream, but the conviction with which she spoke when added to rest of what had happened persuaded them to take Elinor at her word. After all, she had no cause to lie.

Finally, the hunt for answers to the Mournsby Curse could begin. It was Rick who rather unexpectedly came up with a solution as to where to look out information regarding the past. The most likely and reliable source would be the local history section at the library in town. Unfortunately, with it being Sunday the library was shut, so they could not begin their task until the following day. Transport was the next big issue as none of them was able to drive, but by some miracle the village was on a bus route, though the service was far from extensive. Two buses passed through each day, so they had to be sure they caught one.

Emma asked if Elinor was coming too, and as tempting as it was to spend a day in the real world far from Mournsby with its ghosts, nightmares and house breaking shadows, she had research of her own to do. She could have done it over the course of Sunday, but as it involved poking about in the family documents, such activities would attract the curiosity of her aunt. No, she had to do it in private and so she was required to stay at home.

By the time they had made their plans, the lack of sleep finally took hold of the three of them, and as the rest of the village stirred to life, they floated off into the realm of dreams, where they remained until well after lunch.

When they did wake, Emma and Rick quickly left End Cottage in order to spend the rest of Sunday afternoon with their grandparents. They hoped the gesture would be enough to secure permission for their intended venture into town the following day, but when asked by Elinor what they'd do if their request was refused, with a shrug of his shoulders, Rick said,

"We'll go anyway." Elinor likewise intended to spend the rest of the day attempting to secure as much good-will as she could with Sarah, by offering to take Sophie out for the afternoon, but she was too late. Having seen her friends off, she went out to the back garden where her aunt was busy weeding the flower beds.

Sophie was conspicuous by her absence, and as she asked Sarah where her cousin was, Elinor suspected she already knew. Apparently, an hour or two before Elinor came down from her room, Sophie, who had been playing in the front garden, came to her mother and said Mrs Barrowhyde had been passing by, and seeing her without a playmate, asked if she would like to come to her house again. Sarah, although free from work, had lots of jobs to do about the house, and so happily agreed to her daughter's request. Elinor was distinctly uncomfortable with the thought, and quickly came up with an excuse to fetch Sophie home.

Pretending she was concerned about taking advantage of the elderly woman, and since she was up, Elinor asked if it might not be best for her to go and collect her cousin rather than abuse Mrs Barrowhyde's generosity. Sarah, though surprised by Elinor's keenness to babysit, thought the idea a good one, and apparently did not detect any hint of ulterior motive in her niece's offer, which was lucky for Elinor.

On her way to Larchend, a journey she did not savour one bit, Elinor wondered what sort of reception she would get this time. On her last call, apart from Sophie proving difficult to locate, Mrs Barrowhyde had not only been less than welcoming, she had been down-right rude. What awaited Elinor this time?

Sarah had made no mention of a time when Sophie had to be back home by, yet as Elinor reached the edge of the driveway leading down to the house at Larchend, who should be there but Mrs Barrowhyde with a somewhat quiet Sophie.

"Time to go," Mrs Barrowhyde commanded and without resistance, Sophie stepped over to her cousin, took her hand and turned towards home. "I'll see you soon," the woman added as with a hasty bid of thanks, Elinor led the way back to End Cottage.

Sophie remained distant the whole way home, and was not her usual self until after supper, but her behaviour was missed by her mother, something almost as strange as the silence coming from the child. Elinor alone seemed to be aware of the change, and her eyes were unable to break themselves free from the small toy figure, which Sophie stroked constantly as they ate. Her annoyance at being prevented from going into town the next day with Rick and Emma changed to relief as she observed the subduing effects Mrs Barrowhyde's care had on Sophie. At least with her being at home there would be no cause for the youngster to go to Larchend.

It was ridiculously early the next morning when Elinor escorted Rick and Emma to the bus stop. Her presence there was two-fold. She may well have been used to getting up at dawn, but her friends generally slept in until late morning, so it was down to Elinor to make sure they were up in time to catch the bus. Secondly, she wanted to remind them what they should keep an eye open for.

"You're looking for stories relating to suspicious deaths, missing children and, most importantly, the family history of the Barrowhydes. I don't know why, but they keep cropping up, and are the only connection between the past and the present events in the village. Besides that, anything that strikes you as odd, make a note of it."

"Yes, sir!" Rick gave a mock salute as Elinor issued her orders. "What are you going to do while we trawl through mountains of papers?"

"Me? I've got a date in the cellar of End Cottage."

Her friends had no idea what she was on about.

"The cellar is where the old paperwork is stored away. My visitor at the mausoleum said I was an important part of what's going on, so it follows my own past needs checking out, especially as it is such a confusing one."

Elinor's final remark confused the other two further, for she had not yet revealed to them the full sadness of her past, but as the bus was pulling up, there was no time to go into it then either.

"We'll meet you here later," Emma said as she hopped on board behind her brother. "See you about five." Wishing each other good luck, they waved their farewells as the bus carried Emma and Rick to town, leaving Elinor in Mournsby where she had the less than enviable task of delving into her own past.

Waiting until Sarah was safely on her way to work and with Sophie still asleep in bed, Elinor grabbed a torch, descended the narrow flight of stairs leading to the depths of the property and looked about in resigned desperation. The boxes seemed to go on without end. They were stacked several layers high in places and stretched out across the floor as far as her light allowed her to see. It was going to be a long, not to mention tedious task. Having tracked down the light switch, the bulb, which provided little more illumination than her hand held beacon had given, showed the hunt might not be as long winded as she initially thought.

The boxes were labelled, detailing the contents each one held within. Ignoring those which would clearly be of no use, such as spare kitchen utensils, toys and ornaments, Elinor pulled the three most likely candidates to one side and began.

The first box yielded nothing of use. It was full of papers and photos relating to Sarah's marriage, files of old household bills and car documents. Why she had held onto these, Elinor did not know. The second box was a little more helpful, but there was still virtually nothing relating to Elinor other than a few photos taken on family holidays or days out, though these too were comparatively recent. Elinor was beginning to wonder if she had any past at all, there was so little information about her early life, but as she was on the verge of giving up, one small, almost insignificant detail, made her stop dead.

She was grappling with a rebellious pile of papers, which kept slipping out of her hands, when a single photo fluttered off on its own. With a groan of frustration, Elinor reached down to pick it up. Her head spun as the clue revealed itself to her, but it was not the one she had been expecting.

The photo was of a group of six people, all close in age, at a celebration of some kind. She picked out Sarah at once and next to her the Miserable Max she went on to marry. On the other end of the line were her adoptive parents, Eve and Ben, but who were the other couple? She looked at them closely, for there was something in their features. It struck her how alike the unknown woman and Ben were to one another. A thrill of happiness ran through Elinor as an idea as to her identity entered her mind. Was it possible? Could it really be her?

Shaking, she turned over the picture, hoping against hope someone had had the foresight to label image. They had, and it was. The previously unnamed lady was Caroline Carlton, the only sibling of her adoptive father, Ben, and therefore, her mother. The photo had been taken on the night of her engagement party to Patrick Williams, presumably the man beside her, which made him Elinor's father.

It was the first time she had seen a picture of her birth parents. Though she had always known how they died, and that her uncle and his wife had adopted her, nothing had ever really been said about Caroline or Patrick, and it was only now Elinor discovered the void this lack of information had left in her life. She was caught off guard as silent tears streamed down her face as she beheld the happy, carefree faces. It struck her how much in love her parents appeared to be, more so than even Ben and Eve, who were considered by everyone to be the essence of true love itself. Sarah and Max too looked unrecognisably joyous. And what had become of them all?

Tragedy itself was depicted in that small image. Patrick and Caroline died in an accident, Ben was murdered, Eve committed suicide, and Sarah and Max hated each other so much they had divorced. What had they done to fall foul of so terrible a curse? Surely, there had to be some deeper, not to mention darker reason for such sufferings to befall such a small and intimately connected group? There was but one she could think of. It was her. She had entered the lives of each of the three couples and bought death and destruction with her.

She dabbed the drops of salty water off the precious image, struggling to accept the idea, when she recognized something she had seen quite recently. Upon the ring finger of her mother's left hand was gold ring with a brilliant red stone set in its centre. It was the exact same ring worn upon the hand of the spectre reaching for her in one of her dreams. But, if that was the case what did it mean?

Tucking the photo into her pocket, Elinor continued to speed read the papers. Towards the bottom of the stack she came found some paintings she had done as a youngster, probably when she was no older than Sophie was now. There were multi-coloured gardens, three legged dogs and, for reasons she could not understand, many drawings of what looked to be a children's toy house. Considering her widely acknowledged loathing for them, it struck her as being queer that she should have painted so many pictures of one. And it was one house. The same one drawn over and over. She put the papers away and perused the remaining photos though nothing else came to her attention.

Max had been right all along. Elinor was the cause of his and Sarah's problems. Whether or not people believed there was anything more than a series of sad incidents which had left

Elinor an orphan, there was no denying she appeared to be something of jinx, a jinx which left her without a single blood relation in the world. She was truly alone.

Sophie, who had slept in late, called out to her cousin, as she was unable to find anyone in the house. Quickly shoving the papers away, Elinor shouted back to reassure her she was there, and then darted back up to the ground floor, leaving her haunting past in the dank misery of the cellar.

The little girl was back to her old self, but still carried the eerie doll with her constantly. Having eaten a mountain of toast, Sophie asked if Elinor would take her out to play. Elinor was more than happy to oblige. It was a relief to see her cousin back to normal and wanting to do something other than go to Mrs Barrowhyde's, but her willingness to oblige was also a selfish one. Elinor wanted forget, however briefly, the grief Mournsby had enveloped her in. She could see for the first time why people said you should never look back. Sadly, she had been given no choice. She had been specifically told to look to the past, not that she could understand why yet. All she had discovered so far was that death followed in her wake and she was without a living relative anywhere in the world.

Packing up a picnic for the two of them, Elinor, Sophie and the always present mini toy figurine, headed off into the country beyond the boundaries of the village.

The day was beautiful. The weather was bright, warm but with a cooling breeze that meant the sun did not become unbearably hot. They walked through the woods and had their packed lunch sat next to a bubbling stream, which gurgled through the fields as it made its way towards the distant river.

After spending the afternoon looking for local wildlife, Elinor reluctantly took the decision to head for home. Emma and Rick would soon be back from the library, and as much as she wanted to avoid raking up more horrors, she had set out on a path from which she could not turn back, but not even the thought of her friends might have uncovered was enough to spoil the joy of such a delightful summer day. Elinor savoured the moment of tranquillity which would soon give way to the approaching storm.

The made it back to Mournsby later than planned, and as the bus was due within minutes of their return, Elinor decided to abandon her plans to drop their bags off at the house before meeting it. To take up the remaining spare time, Elinor took Sophie to the village shop to treat her to a few sweets by way of finishing off the day.

Leaving Sophie to make her selection, Elinor picked up a few groceries they had run out of and was in the process of paying Mr Braxton, when his wife saw Sophie playing with her doll. There was a distant look of recognition in her eyes, as if she had seen something similar before, but was unsure where. Almost as soon as it appeared, the expression faded, and Mrs Braxton went back to stacking the jars of jam she had been unpacking.

"That's a sweet little thing you've got there," Mr Braxton remarked as Sophie swept the doll's hair back into a small pony tail. "What is it?" Sophie lifted the perfectly crafted copy of herself up to the counter top.

"It's my own special toy. It was given to me so that when I get to play with the house, I have my own doll to move into it."

The sound of breaking glass echoed around the tiny shop as the jar Mrs Braxton had been pricing up dropped from her hand and shattered over the floor. The reaction caught everyone's attention. Sophie's words had had such an effect on her she could focus on nothing else.

"What did you say?" Sophie did not hear the question, and neither did she see the look of sheer fright on Mrs Braxton's face. When the girl did not answer, the shopkeeper's attention zoomed in on the doll Sophie was busy with. Something in her actions, words and behaviour had struck a chord deep inside Mrs Braxton, and it drained the very colour of life from her face. Elinor hurriedly finished her transaction as the traumatized woman staggered out of the shop and into the living quarters beyond.

The sun was still bright as Sophie munched at her lollies, and Elinor awaited the arrival of the bus, but the wind had cooled considerably, and carried the first clouds of the day into view. The scene was perfect in every way, most unusual for Mournsby, and, far from making Elinor relax left her on edge. The calm surroundings were merely a mask behind which some dreadful monster was hiding its real and malevolent intent. Somehow, she felt the threat was building around her and those closest to her, and worried about the trail of death already strewn in her wake, Elinor kept her eyes fixed firmly on Sophie. Nothing was going to get within a mile of her.

Eventually, the bus trundled round the corner of the road and drew up level with Elinor. All day she had been wondering what, if anything, Rick and Emma might find out. She was torn between which outcome would be preferable. Did she want the hunt to move forward or grind to halt? How she wished Mournsby was just an old village stuck in a time warp, and all the weirdness around it was the product of her own vivid imagination.

The idea that everything, from her own misfortunes, to the orbs at night, and lastly to the warning she had been given by the girl who had appeared out of thin air in the cemetery, was linked meant some supernatural force, for good or evil was at work. And Elinor was at the very heart of it. The barely supressed enthusiasm coming from the duo as they darted down the aisle and leapt onto the verge where their friend awaited them hinted their mission had been a success.

"My God, Elinor. When you're right, you are right! You will not believe what we've uncovered." As the bus pulled off, Elinor indicated to Rick and Emma they should keep their news to themselves until Sophie was not present.

They took the hint and were about to make for End Cottage when Emma noticed Mrs Braxton on the opposite side of the road, looking flustered as she practically ran along the pavement.

"Where's she off to in such a hurry?" Emma queried aloud, almost choking on her own hair as the wind rose dramatically.

At the same time the sky lost its summer cheer, donning a cloak of ashen grey as the storm, which had been circling the village unleashed the tempest within. Elinor pulled Sophie towards her as debris tumbled at speed down the road, and the four of them drew nearer to one another as they battled to remain upright in the unexpected gale.

Mrs Braxton continued to hurry on in spite of nature conspiring to stop her, and seeing Elinor seemed to increase the urgency with which she walked.

"Elinor! I must speak with you. It's about…" The last words were drowned out by the din coming from the wind as it fought its way through the branches of the trees along the road side, one of which was groaning with agony at the battering it was taking. Then it came. That awful sensation of old which told her death had marked someone as his prize. The branch was the how and, yards away, was the who.

"Mrs Braxton!" Elinor bellowed as loudly as her lungs permitted. "Get out of there. Move!"

Emma and Rick did not have the chance to be taken aback by their friend's words, for as the warning left her lips, the branch let out a wail, crashed down onto the unsuspecting shop keeper at the very moment she drew level with it. Emma turned her head into Rick's shoulder as the wooden weight crushed Mrs

Braxton beneath it. Rick shut his eyes to the scene and Elinor pulled Sophie into her to prevent her from witnessing the bloody demise of the woman, which meant she alone saw the only other person present at the murder, for that was what it was. For the briefest of instants, Elinor and Mrs Barrowhyde's eyes locked onto one another's, leaving the teenager in no doubt as to who was responsible.

As quickly as it had arrived, the storm disappeared and the heavens were clear and blue once more. Handing Sophie over to Emma, Elinor and Rick rushed over to the helpless woman who was lost under the green foliage of the weapon used to silence her, where, to their shock, they found Mrs Braxton, though seriously injured with blood pouring from her head, was somehow still alive.

"Call an ambulance," Rick shouted repeatedly until one of the locals heard his cries and did as requested. Elinor helped him to lift the branch off its victim, and saw that, as the street filled with those who lived nearby but had missed the accident came out to offer assistance, one resident was curiously missing. Mrs Barrowhyde was gone, her work complete. As older, more prepared people took control of the situation, Rick grabbed Elinor by the arm and took her to one side.

"Okay," he whispered, not wanting anyone else to hear his words, "I'm convinced. It's time we sorted out what on earth is going on here."

Chapter Eleven

The Full Story

"What could she have wanted to tell you so that got her worked up into such a state?" Emma pondered in an almost absent minded way.

"Whatever it was must have been important. It nearly cost the woman her life." Whether or not any of them believed a supernatural power was responsible for Mrs Braxton's accident, there was no denying that had she not been looking for Elinor the branch would not have fallen onto her, and she would not now be fighting for her life in hospital.

"Do you think she'll be okay?" Emma continued. Elinor shook her head without hesitation.

"No chance. She's not going to make it." She sounded so certain Emma and Rick did not bother to debate the odds of the woman's recovery further. By some kind of premonition, Elinor had guessed what was about to befall Mrs Braxton, and with everything else that had been going on around their unconventional friend, it was obvious she had access to information they did not.

From upstairs they heard a muffled sob coming from Sophie, who was being comforted by Sarah. Elinor had called her aunt at work to break the tragic news, and asked her to come home early because Sophie was so distraught. Since then, Elinor, Rick and Emma had been by themselves, but had found it impossible to discuss their respective discoveries.

The brother and sister were struggling to deal with the dreadful event they had witnessed, and Elinor was blaming herself for not having prevented it. She had been warned about what was going to happen, yet Mrs Braxton was as good as dead despite her efforts to avert the catastrophe. She was well aware of the questioning looks her companions were projecting towards her as they went over what had happened, and finally the tension proved too much for her. The time had come to reveal to them the full truth behind her and Mournsby's past.

Rick and Emma grew more flabbergasted as the tale progressed. They swept along from sorrow at her losing two sets of parents, to pure fear over her ability to predict approaching deaths, but never did they express any form of disbelief. They had lived through too much, especially that day, to doubt her.

Elinor had secretly feared the confession would cost her the few friends she had, but at the end of her account, following a brief interlude of quiet, Emma leaned forward and hugged her.

"Poor Elinor. What a life. Then, assuming our suspicions are right, none of this is random. It has been deliberately planned with the intention of getting you here, to Mournsby."

The thought had crossed Elinor's mind on several occasions, but hearing someone else put in into words seemed somehow far more petrifying. Not wishing to linger over her own misfortune, Elinor asked how Rick and Emma had got on at the library. Their features brightened as they grabbed hold of the bag full of paper they had obtained on their trip.

"We got copies and printouts of anything connected with Mournsby relating to death, dying or crime, and were amazed by what we came across."

Rick took hold of the first stack of papers Emma pulled out.

"Well, you were right about the whole children thing, and though none appeared to have died here for a century or more, plenty have met mysterious ends." He passed a photocopied front page of an old newspaper to Elinor.

The headline reported there had been no new leads in the abduction of a five year old boy who lived in Mournsby. Three weeks had passed since he was last sighted, and hopes for his safe return had virtually gone. The date on the paper was 1899.

"This was one of almost thirty similar incidents involving missing children from Mournsby. The papers covered the initial abduction well enough, but in the coming weeks the reports grow less and less, and no-where is there any mention of a single case being solved. As far as we were able to make out, the children were never located, not one of them. But, it gets stranger yet."

Emma sat on the edge of her seat as she showed Elinor another document.

"While checking the obituaries for child related deaths, we came across something we were not really searching for." Elinor flipped through the duplicate copies of the death notices she had been given. They were for adults of various ages who lived in Mournsby, but there did not appear to be anything odd about them so far as she could see. Emma was obviously pleased to have seen something her darkly gifted friend had missed.

"You see; died peacefully in hospital. Killed in a car crash. Drowned on holiday. They lived in the village, but not one of them died here. We went over hundreds of these notifications and not one person has died in Mournsby for as far back as we could go. People have been taken ill here, had accidents and so on, but they died elsewhere. Death, it seems, does not come here."

"Did you find out anything else? What about the Barrowhydes? Was there any mention of them?"

"Plenty. It turns out the Barrowhydes were extremely wealthy, but not greedy. They spread their money about, helping out many local good causes. There were snippets about their generosity in many papers, but the one which really stuck out, and showed how kind they were, was the saddest story we read."

Rick discarded paper after paper as he looked for the items he sought.

"The Barrowhydes had a married couple in their employ, unusual for the time, but so were they. One day, when they were on a servant's trip, the husband and wife were killed when the bus they were travelling in crashed. They had an infant child, a girl, who was left without a living relative. The Barrowhydes, who had a daughter of their own, adopted the orphan to bring up as their own.

"After that, the Barrowhyde family continued to make appearances in the papers when they attended charity events or made presentations, but they came back into the headlines when disaster struck. The girl they adopted died in a terrible accident. She was playing hide and seek with her elder sister, and had gone up to the attic rooms of the house, when she fell and hit her head, killing her instantly. Oh, here they are."

Rick pulled out several documents and passed them over to Elinor, who did not take too great an interest in them initially, but as the years went by and the young Barrowhyde children grew up, she became totally absorbed by the photos, so much so, she hardly heard Rick as he continued to speak.

"Their misfortune did not end there either. A few years after, the husband had a massive heart attack and months later the wife died too, apparently from a broken heart. Erm, are you listening to me?"

Seeing Elinor was distracted, Rick was annoyed that having spent the day stuck indoors doing research on her behalf she was not paying attention to him.

"I heard you. That ties in with the dates on the mausoleum. What doesn't fit in is this."

"What?"

Elinor lifted her head up from the papers, looking pale with shock.

"What is it Elinor?"

"Do you believe in ghosts?" Rick sank back in his chair.

"Had you asked me that yesterday, I'd have said no. Today, my answer has to be, why not? What makes you ask?"

"Because I've seen one." She moved over to the spare seat between Rick and Emma. "These pictures of Clan Barrowhyde. Look at the last one taken before disaster struck. There's the husband, the wife and the two daughters, their own on the left, the adopted girl on the right." Elinor pointed to the older girl. "That's who I spoke to in the cemetery the other morning, the one who showed me where I was to begin my search."

Emma and Rick leaned in over the paper.

"Are you sure?"

"I'm hardly likely to forget, am I? I'm telling you, that is the same girl. Elspeth Barrowhyde," she read the name from the caption under the image. "The one Barrowhyde to have survived the demise of Mary. But how on earth could she have been in the graveyard with me, and still look as she did 1874?"

They had reached a dead end. The papers had uncovered the secret of Mournsby's lost children, and given them an insight into the Barrowhydes, but they had come up with nothing that was of any real help to them. Elinor however, was sure she had missed something. The friends went over and over the papers but nothing new came to light. They would have gone on like that all night had it not been for the phone ringing.

Elinor guessed before she picked up the receiver what it was in relation to. The voice on the other end was that of Rick and Emma's grandmother. Her husband had gone with Mr Braxton to the hospital and waited as the doctors tried to save the injured woman. They had been unsuccessful. Mrs Braxton died an hour after being taken in. The blow to her head had crushed her skull, causing serious damage to her brain. Rick and Emma were wanted back at their grandparent's as soon as possible. Reluctantly, they packed their things up and went home leaving Elinor the information they'd obtained from the library.

Having broken the news to her aunt, Elinor, armed with her papers went to the seclusion of her room and trawled through them again. She failed to find any additional pieces of information in the text, but did see something they'd overlooked in the pictures.

Following their adoption of the orphaned child, the Barrowhyde's daughter, Elspeth, grew more sullen with each passing year, until she looked the very soul of depression. But, in the photo taken after the death of her sister she was smiling. It was a genuine grin of pure satisfaction, and quite took Elinor's breath away. She could not believe she was looking at the same gentle creature from the graveyard.

She thought over everything that had a habit of recurring in the hope of finding a fresh point of view from which to tackle the problem. There were the orbs of light, but there was little she could do to investigate them. During her trip to the cemetery she'd seen nothing to indicate where their point of origin might be. There was Mrs Barrowhyde. Rick and Emma had managed to expose what information there was relating to her, and as much as she needed looking at in more detail, Elinor had no idea how it could be done. She was blocked at every turn for the present. Mrs Barrowhyde would have to wait, as would the truth about the missing children. Was there any clue in the nightmare she was visited by on a nightly basis?

Elinor recited the verse a piece at a time.

"A grey shroud of sorrow, of loss and of pain, shall cover the village bearing grief's name." That line referred to Mournsby.

"Unending, unbroken, the innocent cries shall silent remain, until deaths grace returns there again." Supposing the papers were accurate and no-one had died in the village for years, death had been absent for some time and Mournsby awaited its coming.

"With a touch of a hand, the gates they will part, a beginning to the end of shadow and dark." That was not so simple to work out, but working on the principle everything was connected, Elinor thought it through logically.

One set of gates had featured prominently since her arrival, and they were those of the cemetery. This was seemingly confirmed by the fact that the stiff lock had opened in her hand. For weeks, Elinor had been tormented by the dream, always waking before it finished sharing the story with her. Had the answers to her questions been with her all along? She had to find out, and the only way that could be done was by seeing the nightmare through to its end.

Knowing it was her instinct of self-preservation which caused her to wake, Elinor had to come up with a way to subdue her desire to escape the dreamscape she entered in to. She had to stay asleep at all costs, and she had an idea how to do it.

Tip-toeing down to the bathroom, Elinor unlocked the cabinet on the wall and took out the bottle of sleeping pills her aunt's doctor prescribed at the time of her divorce. She took two of the tablets and bid a quick retreat back to her room. There was no going back. Nothing could disturb her that night. She turned off every light, drew the curtains and settled down on her bedclothes and waited.

Without realizing it, Elinor found herself transported from one world to the other, though the settings were identical. She remained firm in her determination as the dream began as usual, but for the first time she felt prepared for whatever lay ahead. Her invisible companion was there as ever to show the way.

> "A grey shroud of sorrow,
> of loss and of pain,
> shall cover the village bearing grief's name."

The gates appeared before her, rattling in the wind. Without hesitation, she lifted her hand, and took hold of the lock.

> "With a touch of a hand,
> the gates they will part,
> a beginning to the end of shadow and dark."

The lock clicked open and the gates were thrown open. Elinor had been afraid the pills would not be enough to keep her unconscious, but to her relief the dream continued. The voice guided her onwards, picking her up in unseen hands and carrying her swiftly past the headstones, bringing her to rest at the doors of the Barrowhyde's mausoleum.

> "Then journey on through,
> the Keeper of Bones own domain,
> and onto the passage,
> where those who are lost have been lain."

The door to the mausoleum opened, and Elinor moved through them, past the stone coffins to the rear of the chamber where the figure of Death himself loomed into view. She swept on through it and into the passage concealed beyond. She continued through the darkness, travelling more like a disembodied spirit than a mortal being, floating rather than walking. She was briefly aware of the faces of many children closing in around her, expressionless in the gloom, but she was whisked on until she arrived in the hallway of an old house.

> "Beyond lies a danger,
> and many a soul it has claimed,
> who can only be saved,
> when what was taken,
> is theirs once again."

Her journey continued, on up endless flights of stairs until she stopped at the doorway leading into the attic. It opened slowly as she neared, revealing the secret kept within. Set on a table at the very centre of the room was a large doll's house which was an exact reproduction of Larchend itself.

From within its walls she heard the wretched pleas for help as the occupants called for help, as bloodied hands banged on the windows, leaving scarlet prints over the glass.

> "But do not rush to this task my friend,
> for only the one,
> who is born of the dead,
> can break the curse of the House at Larchend."

Stepping over to the house, Elinor opened its front panel to set those held inside free, but as she did so a wave of red liquid poured out as the blood of the victims gushed over the table and onto the floor. At the same time, the hand which brought her to the house took hold of her again, hauling her away from the jinxed toy, back along the same route she had taken to reach the attic until she was once again on the far side of the cemetery gates, which locked themselves against her.

"Now, you know about what it is you're up against."

Elinor had company. Joining her at the gates was the young Elspeth Barrowhyde.

"What? I'm no more the wiser than I was at the start of this palaver."

"You mean you still haven't pieced it together?"

"I guess I'm supposed to help those children, but how? I have no idea what it is I'm expected to do. And why me?"

Elspeth was saddened by Elinor's questions.

"I had hoped I'd be spared having to tell you this, but as all that has happened, and will happen still, is my fault it's only right I am the one who does so." Elinor was at a loss to understand.

"How can you be responsible for this?"

"Because the person who created the terrible curse that has haunted Mournsby all these years, and cost so many people their lives, is me. I am the person who will go on to become the Mrs Barrowhyde you know and must destroy if things are to be made right."

Chapter Twelve

The One Born Of The Dead

It may have been a dream, but the revelation managed to knock the wind from her lungs. How could Elspeth Barrowhyde, the girl born in the 1860s, and the Mrs Barrowhyde she knew, be the same person? Such a thing was impossible, wasn't it? Mind you, if something like that was going to happen, Mournsby was the most likely place for it to do so. Deciding to go with the flow, Elinor questioned Elspeth further.

"You? How can that be? Even if I choose to believe you, how do you become that thing at Larchend?"

Elspeth was unmistakably pained by the connection she had with the corrupt version of herself.

"It's a long story, but I must make this clear. I am not the woman you know. The person before you here, at this moment, is the real Elspeth Barrowhyde, but I was sacrificed in order that she could come into existence. Remember, I told you the first victim is often overlooked? No-one could do the things she has if they were in possession of a soul. She destroyed her human spirit and in its place took a devil-crafted one. I am that murdered soul, and in my stead, Mrs Barrowhyde committed acts that not only violate the laws of humans, but those of life and death as well.

"All these years I stayed close to her, waiting for the day the one with the power to end her bloodshed would come forth, and as a result have been forced to stand-by, powerless, as her victims piled up and life upon life was destroyed.

"But I cannot lay the blame entirely at her door, for the original sin was mine. I was a spoilt, ungrateful child, who so craved the complete and utter attention of my parents that I had no wish to be joined by siblings. Everything was to be lavished upon me and no-one else, but they disagreed and prayed for further children with such a passion that their never being blessed with additions to the family was a physical as well as an emotional pain for them at times.

"That was why they eagerly took in and adopted Mary. How I hated her. She was pampered and cooed over constantly, their darling princess. I was expected to share not only mother's and father's affections with her, but my toys and trinkets too. I was repulsed by the very idea of allowing the beggar child of servants to use my belongings. The final straw came when I was presented with a beautiful toy house for Christmas. Mary was quite taken with it, and was told she could play with it any time she liked.

"I wasn't going to tolerate that. I moved the house up into the empty attic room, the one place she was forbidden to go as it was so precarious a climb. I set it up on the tallest unit there to keep it out of her reach, perfectly aware such an act would not deter her. Mary followed me up there one day, and seeing the house high above her, asked me to fetch it down. I refused, but made a deal with her. If she could get the house down unaided, then she could keep it.

"Mary dragged smaller bits of furniture together and clambered onto the stack of chairs, tables and boxes and made a grab for the house. As she did so, she caught her finger on a loose tack which was sticking out of the roof, lost her balance as she sprang backwards in pain, and tumbled over, hitting her head on the corner of a large table as she went and landed motionless on the floor. She was dead and I was glad.

"I was free of her at last, and had my home, toys and parents to myself again. But that was not how it turned out. Mary's presence refused to leave, and my mother and father grieved for her endlessly. They did not stop talking about the huge void her death had left in their lives. They should have been happy with me, but they weren't and spent less time with my than before. I cursed them, and those who were like them. Why did people have children if they did not want them? Why should I be the only one to suffer? I swore an oath by every drop of blood in my veins that the world would know the pain I'd endured and my punishment would be unending.

"That was it. That was the moment I was sacrificed and Mrs Barrowhyde was born. The first to fall victim to my wrath were those who had instigated the whole series of events which led to my blood vow. I sucked the very life out of them by taking every opportunity which came my way to remind my parents of dear, sweet Mary and how dull it was without her there. They wasted away under the suffering, but in death their pain ceased. I didn't want it to end. The hurt I wished to inflict was not going to be so easily escaped.

"I thought, waited and planned until I knew how to cheat death itself. I drank in the darkest misery so as to be its source. I delved into the most unholy of places and bathed in its mire until I was able to steal the life of another while keeping death at bay. Each evil I acquired was exchanged for a part of my youth or my soul until I was able to appear to those I was to destroy as the least frightening being of all; a harmless old woman. For over a century to those unfortunate enough to have beheld her, Mrs Barrowhyde has looked as you see her today."

"Then why has no-one in the village noticed this?" Elinor demanded, wide eyed with alarm.

"They see what they are allowed to see. You yourself have remarked on the memory loss Mournsby's residents are afflicted by. If she can steal children away from their families, do you think keeping a small hamlet like this under her sway would be difficult? The malignant web she has weaved ensures those who live here do precisely as she wants them to. You, Rick and Emma were unaffected by it because, although you are not children, neither are you adults, and so are caught between two phases of existence, rendering some, but not all of her powers useless.

"Her powers have deepened with each new victim she has claimed, and I don't just mean the children. She has been fed by the anguish of their parents too. They did not know they had even lost a child until they exchanged the mortal realm for that of the spirit one, but still in death they could not be reunited and refuse to move on until they have found their loved one.

"They search without rest for a way to reach them, but until Mrs Barrowhyde's curse is broken they cannot act. The house is the key. The charm is made complete the moment the child sheds their blood upon that object. It happened to Mary and to every soul since. Mrs Barrowhyde claims the lives of the innocents and hoards them away for her own amusement. Death himself cannot defeat her for she worked out a method in which she can keep the children to herself forever.

"She did not kill them. Doing so would unavoidably place them into the hands of the very being she had every intention of cheating out of his dues. She captured their souls and imprisoned the spirits inside vessels to keep them from fleeing. Their bodies were not dead, but they were not alive either and these were concealed in an old tunnel which runs from Larchend to the mausoleum. The house is much older than it appears and was altered greatly by each generation of Barrowhydes who lived there. The tunnel, passing through hallowed ground meant once the children's mortal remains finally ceased to be they were already in Death's care, preventing Him from claiming them, and thus allowing them to move onto the peace of the next world. Mrs Barrowhyde is also beyond his reach. In swapping her soul for all that she became, the human part of her nature was lost, and Death is unable to influence or control those who are not mortal.

"But Death does not like to be cheated and he made a vow of his own. The Mournsby Prophesy. To put things right he swore to send his own child to carry out the work he could not fulfil. The child would be of mortal blood, but in order to bestow the powers of death upon them they had to be born of the dead. You, Elinor, are that child." Elinor wanted to hear no more, but she could not stir herself from her sleep.

"No. You're mistaken. I am not the Child of Death."

"But you are. You know you are, deep down. Your whole life you have known you're different. You just had no idea how."

"No. My parents died in a car crash soon after I was born," Elinor protested.

"I'm afraid not. They were killed in the accident shortly before you were born. Your mother was almost nine months pregnant the day Death selected you to be the bearer of his name. Your mother and father died almost instantly, and you were delivered on the roadside by an emergency caesarean. They saved you, but your life, the life you should have shared with your mother and father, was still taken, and death was given in its stead. You are the One born of the Dead, and no-one else can end Mournsby's grief."

Elinor felt sick to her stomach.

"You have been fortunate thus far. Mrs Barrowhyde has failed to recognize you for who you really are, probably because you did not know it yourself. But she is always on the watch, and knows something threatening her safety is close by. Her search of you and your friend's homes put her on her guard, and though your secret is safe at present, if you keep on refusing to accept the path Destiny has chosen for you, the past will be made present once more."

Elspeth was disappointed by Elinor's defiant head shake.

"Then prepare for the sorrow that is bound to come, for until you do what is required of you, none are safe. Not your family, friends, not even you. Don't be fooled into thinking you are immortal because of your unique heritage. Many lives are on the line. Mrs Braxton proves as much."

The mention of her former landlady's name roused Elinor's curiosity.

"What do you mean? How is Mrs Braxton involved in this?"

"The last child to be taken was her sister, over forty years ago. She went missing when her elder sister was spending the summer at a friend's house. Upon returning to Mournsby Mrs Braxton, as she would come to be, fell victim to the same memory-altering enchantment the other residents were under. Today, something you or your cousin said or did broke the charm. She remembered everything Mrs Barrowhyde had been determined to keep hidden, and it came with a heavy price, one that will go on being paid until you stop her."

Elspeth moved away from Elinor, who, with tears pouring down her face, stood sombre and feeling more isolated from the human race than she ever had before.

"You are the Daughter of Death. See it, know it, accept it. Only then can you set them free." From the other side of the gates, Elinor saw the impenetrable night grow lighter as they approached. With hands out stretched came Mrs Barrowhyde's children, reaching out to her for help.

"Save us, Elinor. Send us home."

Elspeth appeared at the very front of the assembly.

"There can be no salvation for me. I am bound to walk this earth forever. It is my punishment for setting the wheels of desolation in motion, but these souls can be spared. Accept your fate."

The children pressed themselves up against the metal bars of their prison. Their dimly lit eyes stared out of lifeless sockets, bone like fingers tried to hold her there, pulling desperately at her sleeves as Elinor tried to break free, but there were too many.

"Don't leave us here." Elinor wrenched her arms free of their talons, and began to run back to End Cottage, but the cries followed, more pitiful and chilling than they had been before, and increased with every step she took away from their source. She shot a look back over her shoulder, terrified the ghoulish forms were coming up close behind her, but in her haste to evade the children, Elinor collided with a far greater threat.

Mrs Barrowhyde intercepted her on the path, cutting off the way home, and as the moon broke through the veil of clouds which had been shielding it from view the knife she held gleamed in its rays. With a merciless cackle, she plunged the blade down towards the teenager. Elinor felt the tip touch her chest, the first soft trickle of blood run warm over her skin and as her nerves relayed the messages of pain around her body the pills power over her ended, and she woke, alarmed but safe in her own room.

She felt cold and shivered with dread. Every muscle twitched anxiously at the smallest noise, which sounded like an explosion to her ears. She had wanted to know the truth, now she wished she could turn back the clock and unmake her wish.

The room was bathed in light though she had never before felt so encompassed by gloom. Shakily, she got up from the bed and looked at her watch. It was almost nine in the morning. Elinor carefully moved over to the windows which faced out over the fields at the front of the house.

The world was exactly as it had been a day earlier, yet everything had changed and could never be the same again. She had uncovered the horrendous truth about her real nature. She might have been able to dismiss her nightmare as the product of a drug induced coma, but inside her less than human form, she knew it to be true. She was the Hand of Death.

Things from her past which had defied explanation were suddenly easy to understand. She had always been uncannily accurate in predicting when and who death would strike. Finally, she knew why. All those people had died because of her. Her mother and father, Ben and Eve, and last but not least, Mrs Braxton. So many lives ended prematurely just so she could bring death back to Mournsby. How could she find the will to live, knowing she was a creature of destruction?

Elinor looked at the beautiful rose growing in a pot on her window sill. Its delicate white petals were in full bloom, radiating the purity she had been deprived of. Her whole existence was tainted by the realization of what she was sunk in heavily. She extended her fingers towards the bright flowers, but as she touched the plant, she accidentally caught her hand on one of its thorns.

In amazement, she looked on as, for the first time in her life, blood, almost black in colour, appeared at the site of the wound, and though the cut healed itself instantly, the damage was done. The tiny speck of blood fell from her finger and onto the rose, which withered before her very eyes. There was no avoiding it.

"I am the Daughter of Death," she said, with complete conviction in her mind, heart and soul, assuming she had one.

Barely having time to absorb what she had done, the door to her room flew open as hyperactive Sophie burst in.

"Don't you believe in knocking?" Elinor bit in annoyance, but Sophie laughed at her moodiness.

"Mum sent me up to tell you she's gone to work, and can't have you lounging in bed all day. You've got to look after me."

"Surprise, surprise," Elinor said stiffly. "Well, go play with your toys then. I've got stuff of my own to sort through."

"I want to go out to play."

"I'm quite sure you're able to find your way to the back garden without me being there to hold your hand."

"I want to go out, like yesterday. Take me out, Elinor. Please!"

"No. I'm busy."

"Please, please, please, please."

The repetitive chanting caused Elinor's frayed patience to snap.

"Oh, for pity's sake will you go away and bother someone else!" Sophie fell silent, but having given into it, Elinor could not stop herself from ranting on. "I'm sick and tired of being lumbered with. You're not my kid, you know? We're not actually even remotely related, so go find another person to annoy."

Sophie was visibly hurt by the outburst and hurried off out of the room with barely supressed sobs. Elinor immediately regretted her words as guilt was added to the bitter pile of emotions she was already pinned down by, but she was too absorbed in her private cares to chase after the seven year old straight away.

Her reaction to Sophie confirmed her conclusions, or so she thought as she named herself as the bringer of pain, misery and death. How could the likes of her be destined to save the children imprisoned at Larchend? She was responsible for so much hurt, so how could she be the means of ending it? But was she really responsible?

Putting aside her earlier assumptions, Elinor, who was her own worst critic, examined the case from another point of view in case she had overlooked any opportunity to belittle herself, but instead came up with an entirely different conclusion from her previous one. Yes, it was true, providing Elspeth was correct in all she said, that she, Elinor, was the Child of Death, and as such was destined to be the one who brought her namesake back to Mournsby, but was that her fault? The task had been forced upon her. She had not gone out seeking the powers she wielded. It was He, not Elinor, who was accountable for the fates which had befallen those unlucky people around her. Death followed in Elinor's wake, but it was not done out of cruelty, not like the crimes Mrs Barrowhyde had committed. Elinor had been sent to release people from their torments, to help them move on to the world of peace which lay beyond life and death. She was there to set them free.

Able to see the truth at last, the cloud of bleakness lifted and was replaced by a sensation of self-belief and reassurance in what she was expected to do. Eager to speak with Rick and Emma so they could forge the next part of their plan, Elinor decided to collect Sophie from the garden, and by way of a peace offering, take her to see the horses grazing opposite the house before joining her friends.

"Sophie! Where are you?" Elinor called out apologetically as she descended to the ground floor. She had checked her cousin's bedroom on the way down to see if she was sulking there, but found it and the other rooms empty. Downstairs was equally deserted, so Elinor made for the garden, thinking Sophie had gone out after all, but she found only a few birds pecking about the lawn. She went into the living room from which she could see the front lawn. No-one was out there.

"Sophie?" Elinor called again, her voice losing its tone of reconciliation as panic set in.

Where was the blessed girl? End Cottage and its gardens were abandoned by all beings apart from herself and a few birds. Elinor sighed, cringing as she imagined the fuss Sarah would make when Elinor phoned her at work to say she had lost her only child. As she lowered her head in anticipation of the rapidly nearing argument she could foresee, Elinor saw a pile of paintings Sophie had been working on earlier that week, laid out on a side table.

Sticking out from the centre of the stack was one which drew her attention, but not reassuringly. Elinor pulled it free, but almost dropped it the instant the full image came before her eyes. It was of a doll's house, old in style but brightly decorated. She had seen the same house elsewhere, only that one had not been crafted by Sophie, and it was a good deal older too.

Sophie's painting was almost an exact duplicate of the picture Elinor had obsessively created when she had been a child. Indeed, she had uncovered examples of it recently during her search of the cellar. But a far more alarming recognition struck Elinor as she mused over the similarities. It was the same doll's house she had seen in her nightmares, the same house from which soul shattering cries emanated throughout Larchend. It was the House in the Attic.

She knew where Sophie was. In the same way she had sensed Mrs Braxton was in mortal danger she could tell the life of Mrs Barrowhyde's next victim was certainly on the line. Elinor began to panic. What could she do? Calling the police or her aunt was not an option. Her story was hardly going to be taken seriously. They would never believe a woman, who had been alive for over a century, had been wreaking a reign of murderous terror for all that time, and was currently holding her cousin hostage? Elinor knew it was the truth, but even to her ears it sounded like the ravings of lunatic.

Seeking help from the locals was also a no-go. It was highly doubtful any of them would remember who Sophie was. Mrs Barrowhyde had the whole village dancing to her jig perfectly. But she had not taken in everyone. Elinor was not totally alone. She had two allies who, baffled as they were by goings-on, were on her side.

Without bothering to lock the house, Elinor sprinted across Mournsby to Rick and Emma's place as fast as her legs could carry her. Rick and Emma were in the living room and saw Elinor haring in their direction and guessed from the urgency with which she moved something major had happened. With a similar turn of speed they made for the front door to intercept her and both parties arrived at the door simultaneously.

"It's Sophie. She's gone. Old Barrowhyde has her."

"What's the problem? I thought she liked it there." Rick could not see why Elinor was so hyped up over so trivial a matter.

"It's too drawn out to go into here. Come with me and I'll explain fully on the way. All you need to know now is Mrs Barrowhyde's the one who's responsible for Mournsby's troubles. I'm not mad, Rick. Look, please can we go? We have to get to Larchend as soon as possible. Will you help me?"

Moments later the trio were hurrying along the road in the direction of Larchend. Elinor tried her best to explain what had been told to her in the dream and what it meant as they ran onwards, but she was not sure even Emma believed a word of her story, never mind the sceptical Rick. However, there was one point on which no-one could doubt her; Sophie was missing and that was not good whichever way you looked at it.

"Look, you can relax a bit," Rick said reassuringly as they neared the house. "We're almost there."

Sadly, nothing could have been further from the truth. As they arrived at the point where the driveway to Larchend cut into the verge, they were met in its place by an unbroken, overgrown sea of grass which grew right up against a high wall that was identical to the one surrounding the cemetery, and cut off Elinor, Rick and Emma's approach, leaving Sophie trapped on the far side.

"We're too bloody late," Elinor screamed, hammering her fists against the stone barrier as if trying to break them down.

Emma and Rick were too stunned to offer her any assistance, and stood immobile behind her. Elinor cursed herself for having sent Sophie away. This time she and no-one else was to blame for the loss of life which would soon occur. Mrs Barrowhyde had played well, but Elinor was not beaten yet. She was not going to lose Sophie without a fight, and this time she had weaponry to match that of the demonic woman. The game was not over. It had only just begun.

Chapter Thirteen
Death Returns

"What are we going to do?" Emma screeched hysterically, shaking her brother who was likewise lost for ideas as to how they should proceed. Elinor, the one person who had any right to lose the plot, kept her head. The rhyme she had listened to in her dream came to mind. In that, she followed its words and had been led into the house, a house she assumed to be Larchend. Perhaps it would work again. She had to try.

"I've got an idea," Elinor announced with impressive determination, "but I can't ask you two to come with me. It's very risky, dangerous to be honest and more than enough people have suffered because of me already. Stay here, and help if the opportunity appears." She went to leave, but Rick prevented her from doing so.

"Hold it right there," he said sharply. "If you think we're going to let you go in there by yourself, you can think again. We are supposed to be mates, aren't we? Well, friends do not desert each other when the going gets tough, or even crazily supernatural."

"I second that," Emma added. "We're not letting you take on old Barrowhyde without some kind of back-up, despite your being blessed with, well, let's call them exceptional gifts."

Elinor could have argued the point for hours, but every minute wasted in debate was another minute in which Sophie edged closer to her fate, and seeing she had no chance of convincing Rick and Emma to let her go into Larchend unaccompanied, Elinor agreed to take them with her, on one condition.

"You have to do exactly as I tell you to without argument or hesitation. You said it yourselves. I'm in a better position to deal with what may lie within those walls. Will you do that?" Reluctantly they promised, and with them all reading from the same page, Elinor led the way to the cemetery gates.

Rick and Emma thought it an act of sheer desperation on Elinor's part as they beheld the rusty lock and chain.

"No-one's going to shift that anytime soon," Rick huffed, tugging at the shackles, but Elinor proved him wrong. She had accepted she was the key to it all, in more ways than one. Elinor pushed past a defeated Rick.

"It's no use, Elle. It won't budge without the aid of a blowtorch."

"I think differently."

She was right by the gates, and as she reached for the chain began to recite the Mournsby Prophesy.

"With a touch of a hand, the gates they will part." She took a firm hold of the padlock, and as her fingers settled upon it, the lock snapped open, to Rick and Emma's astonishment.

"Bloody hell," Emma whispered as the chain was pulled clear, and the gates thrown wide open.

Until then, Elinor's story had been precisely that, but seeing her skills in action was enough to assure the duo that they were heading into genuine danger. Their resolve to go with her did not weaken, but as they worked their way through the graveyard, they did question their own sanity.

"Look at that," Emma exclaimed with great drama, unable to keep her voice hushed as the tension built. Rick and Elinor paused to see what had caught her eye. It was hard to make out at first, it was that well hidden, but after inspecting the general area Emma was referring to, they saw it.

Half covered by a curtain of thick Ivy that draped over the stonework was a wooden door fixed into the wall which ran along the side of the cemetery closest to Larchend's gardens. Elinor had missed it on her previous visit, but it was so well concealed anyone but a serious observer would have walked right past it.

If it was open they could be inside Larchend within a matter of seconds. Elinor knew this was not the way she gained access to the house, and doubted they'd reach the property in so easy a fashion, but Rick and Emma were by the door before she had the chance to offer an opinion on the subject.

She was right. The door was securely bolted on the other side.

"Damn it."

"Oh well. Back to Plan A."

They continued on along the flattened grass track way until they came to the mausoleum where the family Barrowhyde, supposedly, lay at rest. Once more, Elinor placed herself at the front of the line, rightly too, she thought, even if Rick did not agree with her. Being the only male present, he felt the responsibility of protecting the group rested with him, but secretly, the idea of bumping into Mrs Barrowhyde, dead or alive, scared him witless and his admiration for Elinor, who willingly chose to do just that, tripled as a result.

The doors of the mausoleum parted without a hint of resistance, and once they stopped coughing after inhaling the foul, stale air of the chamber, the teenagers surveyed their newest location in respectful awe.

The thick walls were covered in markers bearing the names and dates of those who were entombed on the other side of the slabs. There were a few small stone sarcophagi sat in recesses to either side and scattered about were statues of angels observing the three friends warily.

In unison, by the sun which beamed in through the doorway behind them, flooding the mausoleum with the golden glow of life, the adventurers instinctively honed in on their goal. To the rear of the sacred space was a larger than life marble figure of The Reaper himself. The statue was dark and featureless as the shadow of his hooded robe obscured his face. With blade in hand, he loomed menacingly above three stone caskets, guarding those who lay inside.

Together, Elinor, Rick and Emma moved towards the memorial with such reverence it was as if they were approaching Death rather than his image. The coffins were clearly inscribed. They were those of Elspeth's mother, father and adopted sister.

"I'm not trying to be a kill-joy, if you'll pardon the expression," Emma whispered respectfully, "but I don't see how being here helps us to reach Sophie. There's one way in and out of here, and we've come through it." Elinor went over the clues she had been presented with. They had opened the gates, and journeyed through the Keeper of Bones own domain. What came next?

'Onto the passage where those who are lost have been lain.' She remembered how in her dream she had passed through the statue and into a tunnel beyond.

"A tunnel. There's a secret tunnel here somewhere. Get looking!"

They tried everything they could think of. Each stone was pushed, pulled and then some, but nothing moved. Elinor wondered if her special touch might hold the answer, but it failed too.

With the sun beating down into the enclosed space and no breeze to cool the air, it was incredibly hot work, and soon the three were dripping with perspiration. Rick took off his fleece jacket with great delight.

"I'm knackered. Here, as you're not busy at present, hold this, will you?" He draped his fleece over the tip of the scythe the statue held high above their heads. It was a comical sight, considering the sombre setting. From where they stood it looked like Death was offering the top to Rick, as if he was a cloakroom attendant rather than the thing most mortals feared above all others. Emma went to pull the top down from the make shift peg with a huff of disgust.

"Have you no respect?" she said, yanking at the top.

The hilarity ceased as a low grinding noise broke out around them, and the scythe Death held began to lower itself towards the ground. Rick snatched his jacket from her.

"You idiot! Look what you've done." The grinding grew louder, reverberating off the stone walls until it seemed to be magnified at least ten times.

"A booby trap!" Emma squealed. Elinor suspected the same, until she saw that, with the exception of the statue, nothing else had altered in the slightest. They watched Death lower his weapon in surrender, and as it reached the floor, a loud click resounded from the wall behind. A small gap was clearly visible.

"I think we have our hidden passage."

It was impossible to ignore the warning the next line of the rhyme gave.

'Beyond lies a danger.' She had to be doubly on her guard from this moment onwards. One false step and she would lose not just Sophie, but her friends as well. She squeezed behind the image of her creator and opened the panel leading to the tunnel. It was pitch black. With it being daytime, none of them had brought a torch, but Rick did have a lighter in his pocket. Taking some of the partially burned candles from the shrines in mausoleum, they entered the passageway.

Three candles might not have seemed like much by way of a means to find their way about, but the darkness around them was so thick the tiny flames burned like balls of fire amid it.

Holding hands, so as not to lose one another, they cautiously shuffled onwards down the extensive, twisting route laid out at their feet. Elinor did not dare to reveal how, according to her dream, they were currently in the area where those children Mrs Barrowhyde had stolen were meant to be. And despite the prophesy advising them not to rush into things, they were doing exactly that.

The soft tapping of their footsteps echoing suddenly became louder, causing Elinor to halt nervously. It also felt to her like the tunnel, which had been stiflingly close, had widened out a bit.

"Turn to your right with me," she ordered. "I think the passage extends out that way. Let's see if I'm right." They did as told, but immediately wished they hadn't. Banging various parts of their bodies on the narrow walls of the tunnel was a delight compared with what greeted them in the newly expanded one.

"Well, I don't know about you two, but I am NOT going in that direction."

Elinor had been correct in her assumption. The tunnel at that particular place widened out into a sort of cavern on the right hand side. It was not a cheery discovery, however. Poking out from the sides of the cave were sections of half exposed coffins and loose bones. Some coffins had fallen in from their original plots above and lay smashed to pieces on the floor."It's a wild guess, but I think we may be underneath the graveyard." This was bad enough to see, but far worse waited a fraction of a candle flicker away.

Propped up around the wooden receptacles in neat lines were rows of children, immaculately attired, though covered in dust and spotted with patches of mould. The clothing they wore differed according to the era they belonged to and went back to the time Mrs Barrowhyde's reign of malignant revenge began. She had been collecting them for some years. Each child perfectly preserved forever, frozen in the moment her curse was made complete.

"They look like wax work images," Emma said, as tears caused her voice to falter.

They may have been immobile, but Elinor was sure each child was watching them intently, waiting. A thousand goose bumps covered her skin.

"Come on. Let's get out of here. This place freaks me out."

"Yeah, and the destination we're heading for is so much more welcoming!"

The girls punched Rick for his remark before leaving the lost children, and continuing on along the passage. They had not gone much further when Elinor's foot hit something raised up above the flat floor of the tunnel, causing her to trip. She bashed her shins, elbows and forearms as she landed on the flight of steps she had painfully located.

"You okay?" Rick enquired as he helped Elinor to her feet.

"No," she snapped as blood oozed down the front of her leg, and soaked into her jeans. "I dropped the candle too. Come here and help will you, Emma?"

By the light of the remaining candles they picked out the ominous staircase as it rose steeply upwards at a decidedly precarious angle.

"Let's take this carefully," Elinor suggested, rubbing her bruised arm. "If we fall on this thing, a broken neck will be the least we can expect." With Elinor at the front of the line bearing one candle, Rick at the rear with the other and a relieved Emma in the centre, they ascended the stairs slowly. It was far from easy. The steps were narrow but high and ran almost vertically at points. All three of them caught the tips of their shoes more than once, and with no hand rail to stabilize themselves, keeping up-right was a challenge, but after numerous stumbles and an equal amount of curses, a chink of pale light not belonging to the candles, came into view.

It was low, about the same level as the floor they walked on, and as she neared it, the source became clear to her. In the glow of her rapidly diminishing flame, she saw something round gleaming faintly. Upon closer inspection she found it was the handle of a door and it was from under this the additional illumination was coming.

"I think we're here," she said in such a tone as she thought necessary to impart the seriousness of their position. It was not needed. If seeing the strange powers Elinor possessed at work, breaking into a crypt, locating the remains of missing children while attempting to stop their murderer claiming another life had not made that obvious, nothing would.

"Are you sure you want to do this?" she asked one last time.

"Just open the door."

Taking that to be a 'yes', Elinor, with quivering hand, reached for the handle. She turned it, cringing in expectation of it creaking and betraying their presence. But the door co-operated with the unannounced arrivals and kept their coming secret.

Peering around the crack in the doorway, Elinor tried to see where they were, and also to check there was no-one nearby to see their exiting the cellar. She could not see anyone as she scanned the dingy hallway the door opened onto, and, convinced they were alone, Elinor, Rick and Emma moved into the grim house. Elinor identified it immediately. The grime coated windows were those of Larchend, though this time she beheld them from the other side of their frames.

It was like standing in a time capsule. The house was, as far as they were able to make out, as it would have been in the days of Mrs Barrowhyde's own youth. The furniture was antique, the décor like something out of a period drama, but she had not kept it that way out of respect for her heritage. The colour had faded out of almost every item and the house felt distinctly unloved, suggesting to Elinor that Mrs Barrowhyde left it in its original state because it either helped with her work in some way or because it enabled her to mock her parents even in death.

"I hate to ask, considering what we've gone through to get here, but what will you do if Sophie's not here?"

"She's here."

"Instinct?"

"No. This."

Without fear of drawing attention to their arrival, Elinor, who had spotted an object in the hall which assured her Sophie was close by, dashed towards it. She trotted down the hallway, past the rooms off to the side and made straight for the front door. Rick and Emma half thought she going to bolt through it back into the mortal world until she bent down and picked up something off the mat.

"This proves Sophie is here."

With a little more caution than their friend had shown, they joined her by the door and found Elinor holding the small doll's house sized figure Mrs Barrowhyde had given to the seven year old as a gift, and which matched Sophie's looks exactly. But as she flipped the toy over in her hand, Elinor saw it had altered in appearance since she last looked at it. The beaming face had been replaced by one of sadness, and actual tears flowed down from the unblinking miniature eyes.

"Come along," Elinor urged, fighting back her own tears, "time is not on our side."

The ground floor was deserted, so they proceeded up to the next level of the house, which also was empty, as was the third floor of Larchend, leaving only the attic space in need of searching.

This was the space Elinor was worried about most. The rest of the house consisted of large rooms with multiple doors and provided plenty of cover if they found themselves in need of a hiding place. The attic offered no way out except that by which they entered it, unless jumping out of the windows counted. Should trouble come knocking up there, they were in serious bother, but there was nothing to be done about it. It was in the attic they would find Sophie, so to the attic they had to go.

Keeping on their toes, for they expected the ghoulish Barrowhyde to appear at every turn, they made the heart thumping climb to the attic. The door to the room was open, but it was as quiet as the other rooms had been.

Could Mrs Barrowhyde be out in the village, hoping to find Elinor before she found the old woman? If she was ignorant of Elinor's real identity she would not have expected the three interfering friends to break into Larchend via the secret tunnel, she'd be more concerned with sealing off the normal entrances to the house, such as the driveway. If so, and Sophie was by herself, they might be able to rescue her and get out of that horrible house before Mrs Barrowhyde knew company had called on her. These and other similar ideas cut into Rick and Emma's wonderings, but not Elinor's. She knew, despite the apparent emptiness of the property, Mrs Barrowhyde was close by.

They pushed the door open fully, unleashing a whine of agony from the hinges. The attic was set up like an old nursery. Toys littered the floor. Shelves were stacked with books, dolls, and teddy bears, all of which looked pitifully at the new arrivals. There was a rocking horse by the window, and a small table set up with a children's sized china tea service, and there, at the centre of the room on top of a table waited Elinor's nemesis. The doll's house she had been haunted by since childhood was there before her, gleaming like new amid the forgotten and disarranged amusements that surrounded it. The house was a copy of Larchend itself, but the terror of her nightmare being a reality was shoved aside as she saw Sophie in front of it, alive if unusually unresponsive.

"Sophie!" Elinor exclaimed with genuine joy, but Sophie gave no reply. In fact, she gave no acknowledgement of any kind. Rick, Emma and Elinor went over to her to see what was wrong. They found the poor girl rigid, as if frozen and though she was not yet cold there was an unnatural coolness to her skin, and there on her finger was the tiniest droplet of blood indicating the blood-tie between child and house was already made. They watched horror struck as the spark of life in her usually bright eyes faded behind the opaque cloud that was filling them as her trance progressed, carrying her further towards the same miserable fate so many other children had endured.

"Look at this," Emma said, as Elinor tried to shake some life into her cousin. It was the sort of situation where, should one of your number tell you to look at something, you did it without question as ignoring them might well cost you your life.

Emma was indicating towards a particular shelf of a large unit near to the toy house. On it were rows of miniature dolls, about the same size as the one Sophie had owned, but each doll was familiar to them. Just as the children had been in the tunnel, the dolls were neatly lined up and each one was dressed to match the child it represented and bore an uncanny resemblance to them.

Emma lifted the representation of one girl down from where it rested. She had long, red hair fastened into two plaits which draped down over her summer dress. Crossing the room to show the toy to the others, she passed in front of the small scale version of Larchend, but as she did so, Elinor and Rick screamed and leapt towards the door. For as she passed the doll's house with figure in hand, the full life sized image of the same red headed girl glided past the outside the window of the very room they were in.

"Put it back!" Emma did not have to be told twice, but as she rushed to put the doll back where it came from, the whole house resounded with a cold, hollow laugh which taunted Elinor and chilled the very bones of all three. They had company.

Elinor had to act. Fast. She shoved the figure of Sophie into Emma's hand.

"Take this and don't lose it," she shouted. "You two take Sophie and get as far away from here as you possibly can. You will have to use the same route we used, but it's the only way."

"You're not going to stay here?!" Rick asked in dismay. "We can't leave you."

"You have to. I've got to finish this. It's what I'm all about. Go! Take Sophie and get the hell out of here."

It went against every feeling he had, but Rick saw it was an argument he could not win, so, deciding he could at least save two lives, he threw Sophie over his shoulder, grabbed Emma's hand and ran out of the door.

Elinor had no doubts about them making it. Mrs Barrowhyde's intentions had shifted focus. She could feel it. Sophie could easily be claimed another day, but Elinor had to be dealt with immediately.

On the topmost floor of Larchend, Elinor felt alarmingly isolated as the sound of the first footstep reverberated throughout the attic level of the house. On and on they went as her enemy drew nearer. Floor boards creaked, each one louder than the previous, then silence. IT was at the top of the stairs.

"There seems little point in my hiding my true appearance from you now," the chilling voice of Mrs Barrowhyde said with barely supressed malice. Elinor had not considered the old lady's physical characteristics being masked in a similar fashion to her murderous nature.

The steps resumed, advancing onwards until she was in the doorway.

The effects of her unhallowed acts were almost too horrific to look upon. Elspeth had spoken of how her evil ways had aged the woman to a far greater degree than was normal, but what shuffled into the attic was more dead than alive.

The outfit she was the same as usual, and the excuse for the bizarre style of dress was at last made clear. She still had on the head to toe coat and her gloves, leaving just Mrs Barrowhyde's face exposed, and what a face! Elinor recoiled uncontrollably.

The bones of the skull poked out from underneath transparent, paper thin skin through which Elinor could see veins of stagnant blood wriggling, and the jaw bone move as Mrs Barrowhyde spoke. Her eyes were veiled in a white mist and protruded forward out of their sockets to such a degree they seemed to be in peril of popping out. Mrs Barrowhyde pulled off her gloves, exposing hands which were virtually free of flesh and whose skin was thinner than that of her face, and they were tipped by long, rotten nails.

The teenager and the old lady surveyed each other, waiting to see who would act first.

"So, you've come at last."

"As you were told I would."

"Perhaps, but I don't think you understand quite what you're taking on."

"Based on the things I've seen today, I've a pretty good idea."

Mrs Barrowhyde was unmistakably pleased by the girl's ignorance. In the hope of giving her friends the time they required to get out of harm's way, while trying to formulate a plan of her own, Elinor glanced over at the replicas of the lost children, and attempted to distract the woman.

"Why did you do this? What was it all in aid of?" Mrs Barrowhyde was more than willing to talk about her work.

"Revenge, punishment, judgement. You take your pick. They should have been satisfied with me."

"Who should have?"

"Mother and father. I was their child. Their first and only born, but was I enough? No! They had to take in that peasant brat. Mary Keene. She was nothing. A nobody of inferior blood, but they made her into a princess. She ruined my life, and I returned the compliment, and took my life back."

"But it didn't work out quite as you planned, did it?"

"No. Instead of spending their time indulging her wishes, they spent it in mourning her, so I was overlooked again. I became invisible to them and I decided they had to go too. But I was far from being alone. I saw there were many more like me, uncared for by the very people who were supposed to love them the most.

"They had to be taught a lesson, and I would be the teacher. I was going to instruct them in the art of pain, a hurt that would go on forever, and not even death itself could break. When their lives ended they would discover what it was they had lost, but still be unable to change it and their suffering would last for all time. I gathered together the unloved children and claimed them for myself."

"How could you do such a thing? Inflict that kind of hurt on people, not just the children their poor parents too?"

Mrs Barrowhyde appeared immune to Elinor's reproaches.

"It was nothing more than they deserved. The children I took were not wanted anyway."

"No," Elinor corrected her, "you made them think they weren't wanted. There's a difference." Mrs Barrowhyde let out another peal of heartless laughter, all the more terrifying as it was now accompanied by her skeletal form.

"Quite right, but children are stupid. And so, we find ourselves with a problem, for you are not a child, and you most certainly are not stupid either, which means there is no place for you in this house."

As she spoke, Mrs Barrowhyde pulled a large knife out from within the folds of her coat. Elinor took hold of the nearest item with which she might defend herself with. She raised the cricket bat in readiness, but the threatening pose did not disturb her attacker in the slightest.

"You have courage, my dear, but let's see how you fare against my children."

Mrs Barrowhyde waved her hand over the dolls on the shelf, and at once they all straightened up of their own accord, breaking free from the curtain of cobwebs they lay beneath.

Down in the tunnel as the dolls obeyed their keeper's commands several floors above, Rick and Emma were witnesses to something just as worrying.

They had made it as far as the section of the passage where the children's bodies were hidden, but as Elinor watched their mirror images jerk to life, Rick and Emma had the less than delightful opportunity to see the lifeless corpses do the very same thing. Their stiffened limbs twitched awkwardly as they responded to the call.

Rick, with the motionless Sophie over his shoulder, pulled Emma into the shadows at the far end of the cavern as the children made for the same stairs the brother and sister had barely finished descending.

"This is a fun house!" Rick muttered as the line of bodies made their way up to the house. He took hold of both girls more firmly than before and dragged them towards the safety of the mausoleum, determined to go back and help Elinor as soon as he was sure Sophie and Emma were safe.

Upstairs in the attic, Elinor heard the tramping of marching feet move unrelentingly in her direction. The dolls on the unit mimicked the action as, one by one, they vanished into thin air, but in their place came a second, much softer drumming. It kept perfect time with those stomping their way through Larchend, but this new noise came from within the doll's house. It was the sound of tiny footsteps echoing from deep within the wooden walls Elinor was beside. Louder and louder they grew, becoming more intense until the toy house virtually thundered with them.

"How do you intend to get out of here?" Mrs Barrowhyde crowed. "The children obey my commands and no-one else's. They are bound in spirit to the dolls and by blood to the house. You may destroy one, but the other will continue. I cannot be beaten. You should have sacrificed your cousin and then you would have lived to see tomorrow's dawn. You have lost all and gained nothing. Your cousin will still be mine, and when you are dead your friends will pay the price for poking their noses in to things which were of no concern to them. I will be victorious again. The children shall be mine forever."

The army of un-dead children, armed with various tools of slaughter, came into view behind Mrs Barrowhyde.

"Only death can set them free, and death cannot touch me."

"No, but his child can." Elinor seized the ceramic figure of clown from the top of a bookcase and smashed it against the wall. She dug the largest jagged shard into the palm of her hand, and sliced into its flesh. Mrs Barrowhyde showed the first sign of concern so far.

"Don't do it. I told you, death cannot touch me. Think carefully before bringing this doom down upon your head."

"I have done."

Pulling the improvised blade through her palm, Elinor whinced as a thick trail of dark blood poured from the wound.

"Don't. Don't do it." Mrs Barrowhyde wailed as her wretched clan surrounded the cornered girl. She didn't waste a minute.

Before the children could slaughter her, Elinor slapped her bleeding hand onto the roof of the doll's house. Her blood soaked into the wood and trickled over its edges, dripping down the windows and walls, and as it did so, the children, who had been inches away from killing her, came to a standstill and try as she might, nothing Mrs Barrowhyde did or said could get them moving again.

"Kill her!" she bellowed. "I order you to kill her." They refused.

Out in the cemetery, Rick and Emma were arguing about what to do next. Sophie was in no fit state to be left unattended, but the thought of Elinor having to deal with Mrs Barrowhyde unaided disturbed them too. They had to find a way into Larchend.

Going back into the tunnel of zombie children was out of the question. The driveway was gone, but there was another way. The door in the wall? It was locked from the house side, but with Elinor fighting for her life, such a small obstruction was not going to defeat Rick. He picked up a large fragment of stone that had fallen from the wall and hammered at the wooden door with all the strength he could muster.

Blow after blow, hammering on and on until, with his hands rubbed raw, one panel split under the force of the continuous pounding. With another strike it splintered completely. He discarded the make shift hammer and cleared the broken pieces of wood by hand, until he was able to reach through the gap and pull back the bolt. Emma and Rick sped into the gardens with Sophie in tow and found they were yards away from the house at Larchend, which, as they looked on, was bathed in a reddish black liquid which was seeping down from the rafters.

"Rick, what's that sound?"

The children in the attic had dropped their weapons as they began to cry out one at a time. As each voice joined in the shrill chorus the intensity of the call built and rapidly turned into an ear piercing shriek of such a pitch, items in the room began to vibrate in its wake. Some juddered across the surfaces they were set on and only came to rest when they toppled off their ledges and smashed on the floor. The walls of the house itself shook as windows cracked, and still the volume of the cry swelled.

With no warning the house was thrown into darkness as they sky outside became overcast. Thunder rumbled close by and lightning shredded the encroaching clouds. Mrs Barrowhyde was furious, and fixed Elinor with a stare of burning rage.

"If I can't have my children, I will have my revenge elsewhere." She lifted her own knife once more, and took a step in Elinor's direction.

The windows of the attic exploded with immense violence, covering the occupants with chips of glass, as a wave of glowing orbs forced their way into Larchend, surrounding Elinor protectively. As they settled, each ball of light changed in size, colour and shape and very quickly Elinor found herself encircled by the misty forms of many ghostly adults, amongst who were her own mother and father, and Mrs Braxton.

The grey protectors filled the room, finally able to confront the monster who had ruined their lives. The house and those within it had been out of bounds to them for so long, but with Elinor's help, the curse which had separated them from their stolen kin was ended, and the parents had come to claim their children at last.

Mrs Barrowhyde endeavoured to find a way past those guarding Elinor, but there was none, allowing Elinor to complete her task. She lifted the cricket bat up for a second time and without the briefest pause, brought it down on top of the doll's house.

"It's not over," Mrs Barrowhyde screamed insanely as she transformed into an ashen cloud and vanished from the room. "It's not over."

The children too crumbled as their remains, no longer bound by the curse, disintegrated. From the split sections of the doll's house, tiny ribbons of pale smoke emerge as the souls imprisoned there were released. Each child drifted over to its parents, and reunited, soared into the air and left Larchend forever. With a swift glance, Mrs Braxton turned to Elinor.

"Thank you," she said before taking hold of her little sister's hand, and they too departed.

Soon only Elinor's mother and father remained. Her mother smiled.

"You did well, my darling girl. You set out to right a great wrong, though the cost to yourself may have been dear. Those families owe you much. They searched tirelessly for their little ones once they learnt how they had been deceived, but as this was not revealed to them until after death, they were left powerless to intervene. You changed that."

Her mother reached out and stroked Elinor's hair sending a cool breeze over her head. "We have watched you all these years, suffered with you throughout your hardships. Many times we have been tempted to reveal ourselves, as we are doing now, but it is something we can do just once, and we knew there would come a day when you really needed our help." Her father stepped forward, and though not smiling, there was no missing the look of pride in his eyes.

"We have to go Elinor. Leave the house as fast as you can. The building will not remain standing for much longer."

With one last look, her parents linked arms and departed in the same way the other spirits had.

A foreboding groan echoed around her almost as soon as they had disappeared from view and a showering of plaster fell from the ceiling, dusting Elinor with flecks of white. The damage she inflicted upon the toy house had been replicated in the structure of the real Larchend and both were about to fall down around her.

Elinor fled from the attic, thundering down each staircase as timbers crashed all around her. Sections of wall came away and broke up as they tumbled over the banisters, missing the running girl by centimetres as she tried to dodge out of the way as fixtures and fitting dropped from on high. The front door saved her. It came away from its tired old hinges as she approached it, allowing her to jump out into the gardens rather than slow to a halt to open it, a delay which would most likely have proved fatal, for seconds after she landed on the dry grass of the lawn, the entire property folded in on itself, and was gone.

Seeing her friends a few yards away, Elinor continued to run towards them as they all moved further on into the gardens where they hurled themselves to the floor as rubble cascaded across the grounds of Larchend. The noise was tremendous, but after what seemed to be an eternity, the destruction came to an end, and silence returned.

Elinor, Rick and Emma hardly dared to life their heads to survey the damage they had done. A tangled mess of masonry and wood lay where the house, a symbol of all that was darkest in human nature, had stood.

"What did you do?" Rick coughed, waving his hand through the cloud of dust which engulfed them.

"You don't want to know."

"What are we doing here?" Sophie's voice was the most joyful thing Elinor had ever heard and she hugged the child so tightly, Sophie was quite taken aback with surprise. Emma plunged her hand into the pocket where she had put the doll Elinor gave her to safeguard, but she found nothing there other than a handful of powder.

The scene cleared and the four examined the results of Elinor's handiwork with awed relief. Mrs Barrowhyde was gone. Her hold over Mournsby was ended and decades of misery were over. Elinor had set all the wrongs right, and the old woman's victims were at peace.

In the coming days the changes to the village became increasingly obvious. Sophie, like the rest of the village, had no recollection of Mrs Barrowhyde whatsoever, and certainly never suspected what had really happen at Larchend on the day which almost saw her die. Elinor, Rick and Emma said nothing to her about it, thinking it better that she did not go through her life bearing such terrible knowledge. The memory loss which had affected every resident, bar those teenagers, also disappeared, and without the evil threat of Mrs Barrowhyde's influence hanging over them, Mournsby became a happier place to live.

Chapter Fourteen
Consequences

"Tara! Come here will you? Yes, sorry Sophie, I'm still here." Elinor repositioned her mobile phone whilst trying to get Tara to join her at the car. "I told you we'll be there the day before the big party. Okay, I've got to go. Speak to you soon. Love you."

Fifteen years had passed since Elinor saved her cousin from the curse of Mournsby, and a lot of things had changed, but many had not.

She was still close friends with Rick and Emma. The bonds they formed during that summer holiday had been forged under such conditions that nothing could break them. Sophie was grown, and in a week's time they were going to be joining her to celebrate her engagement.

Following the events at Larchend, Elinor and Sophie had become much closer and were now more like sisters than distant cousins. Elinor too had seen big alterations in her life. She had married, though she did not do so without taking great care as to whether it was a wise decision for someone like her to do so.

Out of the four of them, she alone had to live daily with the knowledge of what had occurred all those years ago. Had her powers ended with the defeat of Mrs Barrowhyde? There was no way to tell. She was still the One born of the Dead, nothing would alter that, and as such, had to factored into any life changing plans she was faced with.

It was her dark secret, and one she had no intention of burdening anyone else with it. For this reason she had chosen not to have children, simply because it was more than likely with her being the Child of Death, any offspring of hers would also be related to Him. She had been forced to take on a hideous creature in the form of Mrs Barrowhyde and barely survived to tell the tale. She had no intentions of deliberately exposing her own children to similar threats.

Then she met Peter. He was a kind, quiet man whose wife had died in childbirth. Elinor met him through her work as a child minder. Tara, Peter's daughter, was three at the time, and they had just moved into the area because of Peter's job.

It was a case of love at first sight, and a year after they met, Elinor found herself wife to Peter and mother to Tara. They lived in a secluded part of an old market town which only came to life one day a week when the market was on. Tara was now almost six years old, and was loved by Elinor as much as if she had been her own child.

Putting her phone away, and shutting the car door, Elinor called to Tara once again.

"If you don't come in this minute, you can forget going for your riding lessons tomorrow afternoon." It was the one threat which worked every time. Tara hurried back to the house, almost knocking the shopping bags out of Elinor's hand in her haste, and waited patiently by the front door.

She walked to the house, unlocked the door and stood clear as Tara barged her way into the hall, dumping her bag by the table as she continued on into the kitchen. She lowered the shopping to the floor with a sigh, and tutted as she spotted a small toy lying on the mat by her feet.

"You need to watch where you leave your things, Tara," she called. "I nearly stepped in this one." Tara poked her head out of the kitchen.

"It's not mine. I don't like dolls. They frighten me."

Elinor could have laughed at the statement, which reminded her of how she had felt as a child about such things, but something in the girl's words struck a nerve, and it worried the woman.

She moved into the living room as she took the time to check the toy more closely. If it was a 'swap' Tara had made with a school friend, she wanted to keep it safe until the children inevitably wanted their own items back.

A choking sob of utter desperation erupted uncontrollably from Elinor's body as she beheld the doll. It was a perfect miniature representation of her step daughter, Tara. Every curl of her hair, the tint of her deep blue eyes, all were exact copies of those features the child in the kitchen possessed. Elinor trembled to her very core as she clutched the doll, her head whirled as her logical side tried in vain to deny the truth of what it meant, but which she knew beyond doubt to be real.

So absorbed was she in these thoughts, that Elinor in her terror did not notice immediately her reactions were being monitored with interest.

A chill of impending misfortune stole the warmth of her blood and she lifted her head as tears of despair trickled down her cheeks.

From the corner of her eye, she saw her. Out through the bay window, patiently waiting by the edge of the lawn was the figure of an elderly lady, dressed head to toe in black clothing, and the words, uttered many moons ago, and their true meaning, came back to haunt Elinor. 'Death cannot touch me. Think carefully before bringing this doom down upon your head.' Elinor spun around, ready to confront her enemy, but as she did so the woman vanished, leaving nothing behind except the doll and with it a promise of what was to come.

The End

2171866R00078

Printed in Great Britain
by Amazon.co.uk, Ltd.,
Marston Gate.